Jan

This should not be happening. She should not be here like this with him. It was wrong, dangerous. She would be hurt again the way she had been before.

The words ran through Win's brain like a refrain, but her body had slipped her mind's control. With frightening clarity she perceived a truth that she had successfully concealed from herself for years.

She still loved him.

PENNY JORDAN was constantly in trouble in school because of her inability to stop daydreaming—especially during French lessons. In her teens, she was an avid romance reader, although it didn't occur to her to try writing one herself until she was older. "My first half-dozen attempts ended up ingloriously," she remembers, "but I persevered, and one manuscript was finished." She plucked up the courage to send it to a publisher, convinced her book would be rejected. It wasn't, and the rest is history! Penny is married and lives in Cheshire.

Penny Jordan's striking mainstream novel *Power Play* quickly became a *New York Times* bestseller. She followed that success with *Silver*, *The Hidden Years*, *Lingering Shadows* and *For Better For Worse*.

Don't miss Penny's latest blockbuster, *Cruel Legacy*, available in late 1995.

Books by Penny Jordan

HARLEQUIN PRESENTS PLUS
1599—STRANGER FROM THE PAST
1655—PAST PASSION
1719—A MATTER OF TRUST

HARLEQUIN PRESENTS
1552—SECOND-BEST HUSBAND
1625—MISTAKEN ADVERSARY
1673—LESSON TO LEARN
1705—LAW OF ATTRACTION

PENNY JORDAN
Tug of Love

Harlequin Books

TORONTO • NEW YORK • LONDON
AMSTERDAM • PARIS • SYDNEY • HAMBURG
STOCKHOLM • ATHENS • TOKYO • MILAN
MADRID • WARSAW • BUDAPEST • AUCKLAND

ISBN 0-373-11734-5

TUG OF LOVE

Copyright © 1992 by Penny Jordan.

First North American Publication 1995.

CHAPTER ONE

'WIN, what's wrong?'

Winter looked up guiltily from the mug of coffee she was nursing, well aware that she had not been concentrating on her friend's chatter.

She and Heather had known each other for almost ten years now. They had met when they both started taking their toddler sons to the same playgroup, and it was this initial meeting which Heather was discussing now, suggesting that they make arrangements to celebrate the tenth anniversary of the day they had first met.

'We'll go somewhere really special,' Heather had been saying. 'Not the hotel—not with you working there.'

And Winter had known from the way Heather's voice had changed that she had not only been thinking of Winter's work at the hotel where she was in charge of the reception and office staff, but also of her relationship with Tom Longton, its owner.

This was confirmed when Heather asked her uncertainly, 'It's not Tom, is it? I thought you and he...'

'No, it's not Tom,' Winter confirmed. There was no point in not telling Heather what had happened, she admitted. After all, she knew that her son Charlie wouldn't lose any time in telling Heather's son Danny about his wonderful news. Wonderful to Charlie, that was. *She* thought it was far from wonderful. In fact, she thought it was just about the worst possible news she had heard in a long time.

'James is coming back,' she said bleakly, then added when Heather looked questioningly at her, 'Charlie's father.'

Heather's face registered her shock, and Winter smiled grimly to herself. Heather's shock was nothing to that which she herself had experienced when Charlie had made his announcement at breakfast four days ago. The words had been delivered in the truculent-cum-defiant tone he seemed to adopt so often these days when he spoke to her.

Perhaps she should have expected this sudden sharp change in him. After all, he was thirteen years old now, not a child really any longer, but it still hurt her that the closeness they had shared when he was a baby and then when he was young was something he now seemed to want to reject.

It hadn't been easy, bringing him up by herself after the divorce, but she had thought that he was happy with her; that she had more than compensated for his lack of a father, especially a father like James, who had shown more resentment and irritation to his baby son than love.

'But I thought he was in Australia,' Heather commented. 'Charlie's been the envy of every other child in his class since he spent that holiday over there with him the year before last.'

Winter sighed.

'Yes...well, it seems he's decided to leave. I've no idea why, nor do I know why he should choose to come back here.' She gave a tiny shrug. 'He always was ambitious, and he's been very successful. The computer software business he started in Australia seems to have done very well, and I can't deny that financially he's certainly been very generous.' She gave another tiny, unhappy shrug. 'According to Charlie, he's now decided to uproot himself completely from Sydney and to come back over here.'

'Permanently?' Heather asked her.

Win shrugged again.

'I've really no idea,' she admitted. 'He and I...we don't keep in touch on any personal level. After all, there's no reason why we should.'

'Apart from Charlie,' Heather pointed out. 'He worships his dad, doesn't he?'

Win winced inwardly at her friend's comment. Heather had never met James. Win had only started attending the mother and toddler group after the divorce, on the advice of her doctor, who was concerned that she was becoming too introverted, too isolated in her fiercely protective love of her little boy.

'He seems to,' she agreed, and then, perhaps because the bombshell of news that Charlie had dropped on her was still upsetting her so much, breaking through the normal constraints and self-control, she burst out angrily. 'Although I've no idea *why*. After all, for the first six years of his life, James totally ignored the fact that Charlie existed.'

Heather gave her a sympathetic look. Although Winter was not the kind of woman to open her heart casually or easily, they had known one another for too long for Heather not to be aware of the circumstances surrounding Winter's divorce, and slowly, over the long painful months when Winter had first been on her own, she had gradually disclosed to Heather the bare facts of her marriage and its subsequent breakdown.

It must, Heather had thought then and still thought now, be one of the most traumatic things a woman could ever have to deal with; to discover that your husband was being unfaithful to you was bad enough, but to discover it at a time when you were still recovering from a difficult birth, when you were exhausted from constantly nursing and worrying about a very frail and sickly baby, and when on top of that you were barely twenty years old and your parents had been totally opposed to your marrying so young in the first place, must have been very hard indeed.

Not that Winter had been sympathy-seeking or looking for other people's pity. She wasn't that sort. Fiercely independent, and in some ways almost too determined to stand on her own two feet without asking others for anything, she had given her confidences as painfully and reluctantly as a miser giving away his gold.

Winter was an extremely private person, a little remote, in some ways, her manner slightly guarded—but then after the way she had been hurt it was no wonder.

Knowing her so well, Heather was not really surprised she had not married again, despite the fact that she was so attractive. Plenty of men had been interested in her, but she had never reciprocated that interest, until she had taken that course at college and then got her present job with Tom Longton.

No one had been more surprised than Heather when Winter first started accepting Tom's dates. She had been going out with him for several months now, almost a year, in fact.

At first when Tom had bought the dilapidated Georgian house on the outskirts of town and announced that he intended turning it into a first-class small country hotel, complete with leisure club facilities, everyone had laughed at him, claiming that there was simply not the call locally for that sort of thing.

But they had reckoned without Tom's determination, and without the new spur of the motorway which brought so much traffic and so many potential and discerning clients within easy reach of the hotel, and now Tom was talking about expanding, adding on extra bedrooms and buying up land for the creation of a championship golf course.

Winter rarely discussed Tom's plans, even with her, her closest friend, but Heather knew that she must be aware of them. Would she marry Tom? They made a good couple, and Tom, although inclined to be slightly aggressive and perhaps a little more volatile and enthusiastic and perhaps even a little thoughtlessly arrogant in the way he compared himself and his achievements with those who were less successful, did genuinely care about Winter.

But not Charlie?

Heather often wondered if Winter was aware of the resentment and dislike that existed between her son and her employer-cum-boyfriend. If she was, she never mentioned it, and Heather had hardly liked to raise the subject with her. At first when she had seen the worried, drawn look on her friend's face and had realised that she wasn't really concentrating on what she was saying, she had been afraid that some problem had developed between Tom and Charlie.

Sometimes Heather had wondered if any man could ever be as important to Winter as her son. Perhaps because she had only the one child as opposed to Heather's three, or perhaps because Charlie had been so frail as a baby and then so dependent on her once James had gone, Win had always seemed to be much more emotionally close to Charlie than Heather had been able to be to her own three.

She had sometimes envied her that, but, as Win had once ruefully confessed to her, she worried that she might be smothering Charlie with too much love; that she might as a single parent become guilty of over-protecting him, or not allowing him the freedom he needed to develop properly as an individual, and it was for that reason that she had tried to step back a little once Charlie was properly at school and to allow him the space to form other relationships.

In Heather's eyes, Win was a wonderful mother, but she knew Win had always felt guilty about the resentment she had felt when, totally out of the blue when Charlie was six years old, his father had got in touch with her and asked her permission to make contact with his son.

'For Charlie's sake, I suppose I shall have to agree,' she had told Heather bitterly at the time.

'At least, with James living in Australia, he's hardly likely to have the opportunity to disrupt your and Charlie's lives too much,' Heather had consoled.

'I suppose Charlie's quite excited,' Heather ventured sympathetically now.

Win flashed her a bitter look. She was smaller than Heather, barely five feet two and enviably slender, but because she carried herself so well she always looked taller. Her hair was a thick mane of tawny brown which she normally wore severely controlled, sleeked back and tied in her nape with a soft bow. Her eyes always reminded Heather of rich warm sherry, and very occasionally when she dropped her guard and allowed her real feelings to show, as she was doing now, they could burn with an intensity disconcertingly at odds with her outwardly calm demeanour.

'Quite excited? He's practically delirious,' Win told her grimly.

'I take it, then, that his father's return is an event even more exciting than the home team winning the boys' league,' Heather joked.

It was a joke that fell flat. Win looked at her, her delicately shaped face fiercely set.

'If James thinks he's going to take Charlie away from me ... dazzling him, bribing him ...'

'Take him away from you? But he can't do that. You were given custody, surely?'

'Legally, yes,' Win agreed, her eyes suddenly dark and sad as she confided unsteadily. 'Heather, Charlie worships James. Since he had that holiday in Sydney with him, I don't think a single day's gone past without him mentioning his father. If James settles here in this town, as it seems he intends to do... Well, I don't suppose it's any secret to you that Charlie and I are going through a bad patch at the moment. He doesn't get on with Tom. That's my fault, I suspect. After all, he's used to being the only male in my life.'

Win smiled sadly and wryly. 'And let's face it, Tom isn't exactly the conciliatory type. It's a bit like watching two bulls lowering their heads and pawing the ground at one another.'

Heather couldn't help laughing a little, even though she sympathised with and understood her friend's very real distress.

'You're afraid that having James back in the area is going to make things even more difficult between Tom and Charlie, is that it?' she asked softly.

'That's part of it. But what I'm really dreading is James asking Charlie if he wants to go and live with him.' Win saw her friend's face and grimaced. 'Oh, don't think it isn't possible. I know that legally *I* have custody of Charlie, but if James did make such an offer and Charlie wanted to go... Right now he's in the middle of a love-affair with his father, or with the man he believes his father to be,' Win added bitterly. 'He's too young to remember how it was when he was born, how angry James was with me for getting pregnant in the first place. Charlie wasn't planned—in fact he was the classic accident. I'd had flu, and was too naïve to realise that the tummy problems I'd had made my pill totally ineffective. We'd only been married four months, and, as you know, neither my parents nor James's wanted us to marry.

'James was twenty-six, barely out of university and qualified. I was only nineteen. With hindsight I can see why they wanted us to wait, but we were in love—or at least *I* was in love. I suppose with James it was just sex. I was the classic example of an only girl in a family of boys—the only experimenting with sex I ever got to try, with my four big brothers always standing guard, was a furtive kiss or two at the odd party I managed to get to unchaperoned.

'I was so sexually naïve, and I'd had it dinned into me so much by the boys just what their peers thought of girls who were sexually promiscuous, that I honestly believed that the boys—men—really did only respect a girl who said ''no''.

'And that was despite the fact that, had I had the wit to do so, I could have seen for myself that none of my brothers exactly practised what he preached, but of course I'd grown up so much in their shadow, and so over-protected. The male of the species most definitely does have one rule for himself and another for those females he considers to be his responsibility.'

A fact which Charlie was now endorsing by his antagonism towards Tom Longton, Heather reflected as she laughed at Win's rueful words.

'But surely, once Charlie was born, James changed——?'

Win shook her head, cutting her off.

'He was away when Charlie arrived. After we discovered I was pregnant, he got another job, one where he earned more money, but it meant him travelling into the city every day, setting off at seven in the morning and not getting back most evenings until gone eight or nine. He was at a conference when I was in labour.' Win's mouth twisted a little. 'I tried to ring him, but *she* told me he was unobtainable.'

Heather had no need to ask who 'she' was. She knew the story of how Win had discovered that her husband was involved in an affair with his personal assistant.

'No, James never really wanted anything to do with Charlie. He complained that his crying got on his nerves, and I could see from the look on his face when he came home at night how disgusted he was by the state of the house, and me.'

Win sighed again.

'Perhaps if my parents hadn't had to be away in Edinburgh with Gran... If there'd just been someone there to help me with Charlie when he was so ill. I felt so afraid, Heather. People tried to be kind, but the hospital staff made me feel so incompetent, as though I couldn't really be trusted to look after Charlie. He was so small and so frail, and then having that dreadful gastroenteritis... I—I thought he was going to die, and that it was all my fault. I suppose I could have told Mum, but she'd been so angry when I insisted on getting married and not going on to university as I'd planned. I can understand why now, but then—well, it caused a rift between us for a time, and I felt that I couldn't admit that

she was right and I was wrong and tell her how
frightened I was for Charlie.'

'And James's mother?' Heather pressed
sympathetically.

'They were in Canada visiting James's elder
sister, a trip they'd been saving for and planning
for a long time. They've retired there now,
although they still keep in touch.'

'Poor Win. You did have a bad time, didn't
you?' Heather told her, remembering the joy of
the birth of her own first son. She had been in
her late twenties and Paul's birth had been carefully and hopefully planned, just as soon as she
and Rick had felt able to afford to start their
family. Her own mother had been alive then, and
on hand to help and support her, as had Rick's
sisters and mother. Rick had been with her for
the birth, and had taken a month off work afterwards, to be with her and their baby.

'It was my own fault,' Win insisted. 'James
and I should never have married. I was too young
and I was certainly far too immature to have a
child. Perhaps if I'd been married to a different
kind of man, one who was less selfish . . .' She bit
her lip. 'That's what I'm so afraid of, Heather—
that James is going to shatter all Charlie's illusions. Charlie worships him, but he doesn't really
know him, and I'm so afraid that once he does . . .
I know that Charlie needs a man in his life, the
right kind of male influence and guidance, but
for that influence to come from James . . .'

'And you're sure he's coming back permanently and not just for a visit?' Heather persisted.

'So it seems. After all, he *is* the business, and I suppose he can produce these computer software packages just as easily here as he does in Australia. It's very difficult for me to talk to Charlie about his father,' Win admitted. 'Charlie tends to get very defensive and sullen—my fault, I suppose. Sometimes I feel he almost wants me to criticise James so that he can immediately leap to his defence.'

'Have you ever tried to discuss with Charlie the reasons why you divorced his father?' Heather asked gently.

Win shook her head.

'No. I know he blames me for the divorce, though. I hate myself for saying this, Heather, but sometimes—well, it's almost as though I'm willing James to reveal himself to Charlie in his true colours, and yet really that's the last thing I want, because I know how much it would hurt Charlie if he did.'

Heather's face softened.

'You judge yourself too harshly,' she told her, hugging her. 'You are only human, Win, and I know how hard it's been for you. All right, so James left you with the house and never tried to claim his share, and financially he's always been generous...'

'I've never spent a penny of his money on myself,' Win told her quickly, defensively almost.

'I know you haven't, and it can't have been easy for you once James did start to take an interest in Charlie—all those expensive and inappropriate gift parcels from Sydney, and then that trip out there...'

'I think it was that that spurred me into going to college and getting myself some proper qualifications, getting myself a job.'

'But you've always worked,' Heather protested.

Win pulled a face. 'Part-time jobs without any real status—the kind of low-paid jobs that women like me have to take. I suddenly realised how poor an image I was giving Charlie of our sex. I wanted him to see that women could achieve and be successful.' She bit her lip and flushed. 'I suppose, if I'm honest, I was jealous of constantly hearing him saying how successful James was, and, let's face it, working at the hotel can hardly compare with owning and running a successful company.'

'I know you better than that,' Heather told her stalwartly. 'And I also know that the last thing you want for Charlie is that he should judge and measure people by their commercial achievements. You've worked so hard to encourage him to grow in every direction, Win. All those cold wet afternoons watching him play football! I used to get quite furious with you when Danny came back and complained that I never watched him play. And then there's his chess, and his swimming, not to mention the drama group...'

She stopped as Win pulled another face. 'You make it sound as though I'm force-feeding him on "suitable" activities. I just didn't want him to grow up being isolated. You feel you have to try so much harder when there's only you.' Her mouth trembled suddenly, and Heather realised how very genuinely disturbed her friend was by the fears aroused by her ex-husband's projected return.

'Oh, God,' she muttered thickly, reaching for a tissue and firmly blowing her nose, 'I *loathe* people who wallow in self-pity. Now,' she asked firmly, 'what was all this about a celebration? Your wedding anniversary is still six weeks away, isn't it?'

'Yes, but what I was thinking of celebrating was *our* anniversary.'

When Win frowned Heather explained.

'Ten years...of course, it must be. So what did you have in mind?'

'Oh, I don't know—a weekend with Tom Cruise; a fairy godmother to instantly transform me into Julia Roberts,' Heather sighed, while Win laughed. 'No, what I'd really got in mind was a day at a health hydro,' Heather told her. 'It's something I've always fancied,' she added yearningly. 'All that pampering and spoiling—mm. And——'

'Mm, sounds good,' Win agreed. 'But pricey.'

'We deserve it,' Heather told her positively.

Win looked doubtful. 'Charlie's been on at me for a new pair of trainers, and——'

'No,' Heather interrupted her firmly, then added a little more gently, 'You spoil him sometimes, Win. It won't do him any harm to wait a little longer for his trainers. It's time *you* indulged yourself a little bit.'

'Perhaps,' Win agreed, glancing at her watch and getting up. 'Heavens, I should have been at work five minutes ago.'

Heather walked out to her car with her.

When Tom Longton had given her the job, he had also given her a brand new car, a pretty sporty hatchback model which Heather suspected he had chosen especially for Win rather than for purely commercial reasons. Charlie, of course, disliked it, and said so.

'When exactly is he—James—due back?' she asked Win as the latter got into the car.

Win frowned.

'I don't know. Charlie went all cagey on me when I asked him, so I didn't press him. As far as I'm concerned, *whenever* he comes back it'll be too soon.'

As she started the engine, she gave Heather a brief unhappy smile.

'Why is it, Heather, that just when you think that things are picking up, that life looks good, something like this happens?'

Heather's heart ached for her as she watched her drive away, and then as she went inside she wondered soberly if Win had told Tom yet about her ex-husband's imminent return.

CHAPTER TWO

THANKFULLY Win got into her car and started the engine. It had been a particularly hectic and fraught afternoon, with some Japanese guests arriving unexpectedly a whole day earlier than their reservations allowed for. Luckily they had been able to fit them in, but she had had one or two anxious moments.

Normally she loved her job, loved the challenges it brought, loved the people she met, the sense of self-worth and achievement she got from using the skills she had learned. She was proud of what she had achieved, all the more so perhaps because of the way Charlie had so unwittingly drawn a contrast between her achievements and those of his father.

She remembered how she had laughed when her parents had tried to tell her that one day she might regret having given up the opportunity to go to university. How *could* she, she had demanded fiercely, when doing so would mean she would be parted from James?

She also remembered how later, when they were alone, James had whispered to her that he wished she were a little older; that he was not really surprised at her parents' attitude. But then she had reached up and put her arms around him, kissing him in the way he had taught her, and with a small groan he had taken hold of her, kissing her back, pushing her down against the cushions of the settee.

He had made love to her properly for the first time that night, and Win had been shocked and distressed to learn that sex was not necessarily instantly blissful.

James had blamed himself, assuring her that next time things would be different... better. She had been doubtful, still upset by what she had seen as her inability to fully please him, but he had been right. The next time it had been better—better than better, blissfully, satisfyingly better—— Quickly she suppressed her truant thoughts.

Tom's hotel was several miles outside the town. It was midsummer and the grass verges alongside the road were bright with orange poppies. Fitful sunshine dappled the fields, clouds casting racing shadows over the distant hills.

Feeling the tension gripping her muscles, knowing how reluctant she felt to go home and face Charlie's stubborn accusing face, on an impulse Win turned off the main road and pulled into a quiet lane, where she stopped her car and wound down the window. Her head ached slightly from the pressures of her day, or from the fear caused by the news of James's return.

She leaned back against the seat head-rest, closing her eyes and letting her thoughts drift, a luxury she seldom had time for these days, an indulgence she felt she ought to have put behind her anyway. Daydreams were for adolescents, not adult women. As a girl she had often been accused of being a daydreamer.

She smiled painfully to herself. As she had told Heather this morning, until she met James, her life had been a very protected one indeed—overprotected in many ways.

She had been coming out of a shop the first time she met him, and had literally walked straight into him, going over on her ankle and yelping with the unexpected pain. All thoughts of that pain had been driven right out of her mind, though, when he had crouched down at her side and taken hold of her ankle, running his fingers thoroughly and clinically over it, asking her anxiously how she felt. But she had been in too much of a state of delirious shock to respond.

He was the most physically compelling man she had ever seen: tall, with thick dark brown hair and tanned skin. The hands that held her ankle were long-fingered, the nails clean and neatly cut. He was wearing a heavy-duty workmanlike watch and his leather blouson jacket had a softness about it that despite its battered appearance made her want to run her fingertips over it in appreciation of its butter-soft sensuality.

When she didn't speak, he looked gravely at her. His eyes, she discovered, were pure gold like a tiger's. Her breath caught in her throat, the most powerful emotional and physical sensation she had ever experienced in her life gripping her, and she knew instantly that she was in love.

In a daze she allowed him to pick up the shopping she had dropped and to guide her to his car. He would take her home, he told her, and she, knowing that if he had told her he was taking her to the moon she would have simply gone with him, nodded and allowed him to take her by the arm and guide her through the other shoppers to the car park.

As he drove, she learned that he had just returned home after completing his Master's at Harvard, and that he intended to start up his own business in computer software, but that in the meantime he had taken a job locally because he wanted to take some time out to be with his parents before he did so.

He asked her her name and she told him, breathlessly, blushing a little as he repeated it thoughtfully.

'Winter—unusual.'

'I was born on the day of the winter solstice,' she told him awkwardly. Her unusual name had always embarrassed her, and she preferred to be called the more conventional Win.

'Winter by name, but not by nature,' he had said then. 'Not with that warm colouring.' And as he spoke he leaned forward and touched her hair. She had worn it loose in those days, falling thickly below her shoulders and kept off her face

with an Alice band. She'd thought the style
childish and longed for something shorter and
more sophisticated, but her brothers had derided
her, telling her she was far too young to pretend
to be sophisticated, and out of habit she had de-
ferred to them.

By some quirk of fate that summer they were
all away from home. Gareth, the eldest, was in
New Zealand getting to know his fiancée's family,
the twins, Simon and Philip, were backpacking
in the States, and Jonathan, who was in his last
year at university, had gone on an archaeological
dig with some fellow students, and so for once
Win was without her protective guard dogs.

Initially her parents were quite happy for her
to see James. He was older, mature... sensible,
aware of her innocence and youth—or so her
mother later told her they had believed.

Win might have been innocent, but she was
also in love, and she had made no attempt to
hide her feelings from James. The first time he'd
kissed her she had clung fervently to him, winding
her arms around him, opening her mouth ex-
perimentally beneath his and then feeling her
heart thunder in excitement as his grip on her
tightened and she felt the hot eager thrust of his
tongue inside her mouth.

Afterwards she watched him with luminous
dazed eyes that betrayed the effect he had had
on her. Beneath her thin cotton T-shirt her breasts
ached and pulsed, the nipples hard, pushing out

the fine cloth. James touched one lightly with his fingertip, gently rimming it, dark colour surging up under his skin as he told her thickly, 'Next time I shall kiss you there, and then you'll really know what getting excited's all about.'

She had been so desperately in love with him, so completely without any defence against her own feelings, or against the sudden powerful surge of her own sexuality. And there was no escaping from the truth. It was the discovery of that sexuality as much as what she had believed was her love for James that had carried her so passionately into such an intense relationship with him.

She had wanted him so much that quite simply everything else had ceased to be of any importance, and because she had no past experience to guide her she had naïvely assumed that because she wanted him she must love him.

No one had ever allowed her to discover that the sexual urge could be just as powerful in women as it was in men. Just thinking about James made her body ache in ways she had never before even known existed. Of course she loved him, she cried passionately when her mother tried to suggest that it might just be a crush; that being in love was not the same as loving someone; that she was too young to think of committing her life to someone she had only known a matter of a handful of months.

She was over eighteen, and her parents could not stop them from marrying, she had pointed out defiantly.

What about university? her parents had countered. What about her future?

James *was* her future, she had told them.

Even James himself suggested tentatively that it might be better if they were to wait, but she immediately burst into tears, accusing him of not wanting her. He had taken hold of her to comfort her, and within seconds she was clinging eagerly to him.

It had been after the first time they had made love and she had confessed to him that, despite her promise to do so, she had still not asked her doctor for a prescription for the contraceptive pill that James had insisted on not just making her an appointment at the family planning clinic, but on going there with her. A baby at this stage in their relationship, or indeed for several years after they were married, was simply not feasible, he had told her.

'You're so very young,' he had groaned when he saw her face. 'Sometimes I think your parents are right and that we should wait, but I want you so much...'

They had been married two months later, much against the wishes of her parents, a quiet church ceremony because she hadn't wanted to wait any longer to be James's wife.

They had bought a small sturdy stone-built cottage on the outskirts of the town, and for a while, for a very short while, Win had been blissfully happy. James was a tender, considerate lover, gradually allowing her to discover her sexuality, and it was only years later, long after their divorce, that she actually realised how much he himself must have been holding himself back.

He had been unselfish and loving to her then, cherishing her, loving her, laughing when she burned his meals and he had to iron his own shirts. When flushed with mortification and shame, she had asked him if he regretted marrying her, he had taken her in his arms and told her that it wasn't her housewifely skills he had married her for.

'Besides,' he had whispered against her mouth, 'after Christmas you'll be starting college, and you won't have time for ironing and cooking then.'

That had been a bone of contention between them. Win had been quite content to be his wife, wanting nothing more, but he had insisted that, while she might have given up her chance to go to university, that did not mean she could not take a degree course here at home.

'What do I need a degree for now?' she had asked him. 'I don't *want* a career. Just you and our children.'

James had looked at her seriously.

'You're so young, Win,' he had told her. 'You think that now, but one day...'

They had argued about it, but he had been insistent, and then had come her flu and Charlie's conception.

Had it been because she had *known* how he would feel that she had deliberately kept back the news for as long as she could?

When she had finally broken the news to him, at first he had been shocked and angry. Through her tears she had watched him pacing their sitting-room as he told her, 'It's too soon, Win. We still hardly know one another.'

And she had discovered over the months that followed how little she knew him.

He had changed his job, getting one that paid far more money in the city, so that consequently she hardly ever saw him.

Her family, to whom she turned for sympathy and company, seemed to share James's view that her pregnancy was something that should simply not have happened so early on in their marriage.

'Of course I shan't be able to go to college now,' she had said to James, and had winced as she saw the look in his eyes. It was almost as though he had thought she had deliberately got pregnant so that she wouldn't have to go to college.

The first rifts in their relationship had begun.

And then had come the evening James had told her they had to attend a company function. She had been seven months pregnant at the time and feeling acutely uncomfortable; perhaps because she was so small, with her pregnancy, she had become very large, the slowing down of her body irritating and hampering her.

They had ceased making love. Win had been so angry with James when he had not welcomed the news of her pregnancy that when he attempted to touch her she had pushed him away, and now he no longer tried to touch her. She ached for him to do so, but pride wouldn't allow her to find the words to tell him, and a small festering worm of misery suggested to her that perhaps he no longer *wanted* to make love to her now that she was pregnant and so enormous.

And then, at his new firm's annual dinner dance, she had seen the way Tara Simons was looking at him, the way she stood far too close to him, angling her body, her slim, supple, *un-pregnant* body against his; the way she deliberately excluded Win from the conversation, the way she subtly put Win down by mentioning her qualifications, talking enthusiastically to James about their work, a subject which excluded Win completely. She knew little or nothing about computer software.

Win's woman's instinct had told her immediately that Tara wanted James, and just as immediately she had suspected that despite his disclaimers James *did* find her attractive. How could he not do so? Tara was tall, a redhead, with long catlike-green eyes and a sensuality that even Win could see.

The rifts between them widened and hardened. James took to sleeping in the spare room—so as not to disturb her, he told her when she managed to force herself to question him about it.

Her mother had called round unexpectedly one day when Win was on her own. It was a Saturday morning, and James had announced that he had to go into the office. Win had rung him there when she realised he hadn't said what time he would be back, and had dropped the receiver as though it burned when Tara answered the call.

'Win! My dear, are you all right?' her mother had asked her anxiously as Win opened the door to her.

Win had suddenly seen herself, from her mother's expression, as her mother had been seeing her—her hair unwashed and untidy, the smock she was wearing grubby and unironed, her face unmade-up and puffy from her pregnancy.

Her mother's frown had deepened when she saw the untidy state of the sitting-room, and the washing up piled in the kitchen.

She knew how untidy and unappealing everything looked, including her, Win admitted to herself, but she was so tired all the time, and besides, what was the point? James was never there, and when he was... When he was, it seemed to her that he didn't want to be with her. She saw the way he looked at her sometimes, frowning as he studied her, no doubt wondering why on earth he had married her, she thought miserably.

No doubt he would have preferred to be married to someone like Tara—someone who was far too clever to become accidentally pregnant, someone who, like him, had been to university, who had a career. Well, she could have gone to university as well if she hadn't met him.

She had seen two of her old schoolfriends in town the other day, and they had been astonished to see that she was pregnant—astonished and pitying.

With her mother's help, she got the house tidy and washed her hair. Her back ached so much that she was tempted to have it cut short, but James had once told her that he loved its thick length, as he wound it around her throat and kissed her through it.

Tears blurred her eyes. What had happened to them, to their love?

It had been gone four o'clock in the afternoon when James came home. Win had seen the relief, the pleasure almost in his eyes when he took in the tidy house and her cleanly washed hair. He had come towards her, putting his arms around her, nuzzling her ear, and that had been when she had smelled the strong perfume on him. She had become acutely conscious of different smells during her pregnancy, and there was no mistaking this one. It was Tara's.

She had pushed him away from her immediately, her face red with anguish as she yelled at him, 'Don't touch me! Just don't touch me!'

It had been less than a month after that that she had gone into early labour and Charlie had been born, while James was away—with Tara.

He hadn't even *seen* Charlie until he was over a day old. Win remembered how he had frowned at the baby, almost reluctant to look at him, never mind pick him up, and how he had turned away when she had started to feed him.

She had ached for him to show her some affection, to reassure her that he still loved her and that he loved their child, but none had been forthcoming.

She had wanted to have Charlie's cot in their room next to their bed, but James had insisted on banishing him to his nursery. When Charlie developed gastro-enteritis she had screamed furiously at James that it was his fault, that if she had been allowed to have Charlie next to her, as she had wanted, he wouldn't have become ill.

She had known the moment she said it that she was being unfair, but it was too late to call back the words, and besides, what difference would it have made? James no longer loved her; she was sure of that.

Confirmation that she was right came six months later, when James did not come home at all one night.

Halfway through the morning the phone rang. Win recognised Tara's smooth-as-cream voice immediately.

'If you've been worrying about James, there's no need,' she told Win smoothly. 'He spent last night with me...' She paused delicately and then added, 'you *do* understand what I'm saying, don't you, Win?'

Win had replaced the receiver without answering. Sickness filled her body, her head pounded with pain, while her heart ached with the most acute anguish she had ever experienced. She had put Charlie in his pram and walked him for miles, the tears running down her face, and then when James came home she had told him she wanted a divorce.

He had tried to argue with her, but she refused to listen to him, or to mention his affair with Tara. She had too much pride for that—too much pride and too much pain.

She had realised when she'd listened to Tara's revelations just how much she actually *did* love him. Too much, she acknowledged as she kept her back to him and repeated her demand for a divorce.

Oddly, her family counselled her against her decision, pointing out that she had Charlie to consider now, but she had been adamant, demanding that James move out of the house immediately and then refusing to see him.

The sound of a plane overhead brought her sharply out of her thoughts. She moved uncomfortably in her seat, frowning a little. It had been a long time since she had allowed herself to recall so much of the past, to think about it so deeply. Normally the moment any old memories of her brief marriage surfaced she pushed them aside, suppressing them, and now with adult hindsight she was uncomfortably aware of how very immature she had been, how very selfish and spoiled in some ways.

Her frown deepened as she dwelt on this new image of her younger self, surveying it with the maturity and knowledge she had gained in the years that had passed.

Her family *had* been right; she *had* been too young for marriage and for motherhood. Now, for instance, there was no way she would not immediately question the kind of hours James had claimed he had to work; no way she would behave with such childish petulance and such short-sightedness, no way she would allow her pride and self-respect to become so diminished that she neglected herself or her home, no way she would not leap at the opportunity to broaden her horizons.

No way, either, that she would become so totally engrossed in her child that she didn't merely neglect its father, but virtually abandoned him as well.

Win moved uncomfortably in her seat. It was odd how plainly she could see *now* how her own actions must have contributed to the rifts that had developed between them.

James hadn't been ready for the commitment of children. He hadn't *wanted* Charlie. In fact, she suspected with hindsight that all he had wanted was simply a sexual relationship with her, and that because of this he had convinced himself that he loved her.

Whatever the original reasons for their marriage, it was over now, and had in fact never really existed. The kind of relationship she and James had shared was certainly not what she now considered to be the kind of relationship she wanted with a man.

She had been so subservient, so clinging, so *pathetic* in many ways. She would never be like that now. Motherhood had changed her, forcing her to put someone else's needs before her own.

As the youngest of the family, she had been indulged. Her brothers had sometimes treated her more like a pet dog than a fellow human being, she reflected wryly, and that was as much her fault as theirs.

They didn't do so now.

Win smiled to recall how surprised they had been by the way she had changed, by her new authority, her new awareness of herself and others, her calm claiming of her right to their respect as well as their love. No, she would never make the mistakes again that she had made with James the next time.

The next time... Win's heart thumped heavily. She still hadn't been able to bring herself to tell Charlie that Tom had proposed to her. She hadn't even made her own mind up whether or not she intended to accept him.

She liked him; she admired his drive and what he had achieved, even if sometimes his aggression and occasional lack of sensitivity made her wince. What she had no doubts about at all was the fact that he loved her.

Did she love him?

She stared at the skyline. Three months ago, while Charlie was away on a school trip—finding time to be alone together with a sharp-eyed thirteen-year-old about was, she had discovered, virtually impossible—she and Tom had made love.

For her it had been the first time since James. Perhaps it was because she was older, wiser, less inclined to see things through rose-coloured glasses that the experience had somehow not really lived up to her expectations.

Tom had been considerate and caring enough. He had taken time and care, and he was certainly far from inexperienced. She had not expected, as she had with James, that there would be immediate fireworks, but she had certainly expected to feel rather more than she had—a lot more, given her knowledge of how easily James had aroused her.

Neither of them had said anything about it, of course, but she had sensed that Tom was disappointed, and if she was honest with herself it was almost a relief that Charlie's antipathy towards him and constant presence meant that they had not had any opportunity to repeat the exercise.

But then, as she had remarked quite recently to Heather, there were far more important things in a relationship than sex—or at least there were in the kind of relationship she wanted—and Tom, fortunately, had not pushed her.

Perhaps things would get better with practice and custom. But then when did they get the opportunity? Win was well past the age when she welcomed the idea of making love impetuously in a car on the way home from a date.

She winced a little, suddenly remembering doing exactly that with James. They had been out to dinner, and on the way back she had touched his thigh, tensing as his muscles clenched, staring at him wide-eyed, her heart pounding when he abruptly stopped the car and turned towards her.

Perhaps she was just past the age of being capable of that kind of sexual intensity, she reflected as she restarted her car. And if she did agree to marry Tom, would that have the effect of driving Charlie closer to his father? If only

Tom could learn to be a little less hard on Charlie, a little more understanding, and if only Charlie wouldn't always be so belligerent, and if only he would not constantly bring James's name into the conversation whenever Tom was there.

She winced as she remembered Tom's angry comment that he was thankful James was living in Australia. 'If he's as wonderful as Charlie seems to think, I'm surprised you're still not married to him,' he had told her sourly.

'He *is* Charlie's father,' Win had felt obliged to point out in defence of her son.

And when she had tried to suggest to Charlie that it might not be a good idea to mention James quite so often when Tom was there, Charlie had demanded, 'Why shouldn't I? He *is* my dad.'

The problem was that Charlie was starting to grow up and that he seemed to be getting as over-protective of her as her brothers had once been.

Well, she had learned her lesson, and no matter how much she loved her son he must accept that she had a right to her own private life and to her own friends, even if he himself could not always like them. That was a lesson he must learn for his own sake, and for the sake of the woman who would eventually share his life, as well as for hers.

However, it was one thing to get him to accept her right to have Tom as a friend. To get him to accept him as her husband and his own step-father was quite a different matter.

As she drove through the town, she heard the church clock striking, and grimaced. She hadn't realised how late it was. Charlie had been spending the afternoon with a friend. They had been planning to watch a football match on television together. The friend's father was apparently bringing them home.

When she had queried this, he had been quite cross with her, reminding her of how old he now was.

The cottage James had bought when they were first married was still her home. Together with half a dozen others, it looked out on to open fields at the back and had a good-sized garden. Last year she and Charlie had painted the outside, a task neither of them had really enjoyed but which Win had felt had done them both good.

Tom had been horrified. He would have got one of his own handymen to do that for her, he had told her, but she had shaken her head. One thing she had learned was how important it was to her to be independent—a change from the days when she had helplessly leaned on others and docilely allowed them to make her decisions for her.

There was a car parked outside the cottage, an expensive Daimler saloon with new number-plates. Guiltily she parked behind it.

Charlie had his own key for the cottage. Obviously his friend's father had brought him home and Charlie must have invited him inside. She would have to apologise for being late. She only hoped the father would not judge her as a bad mother for allowing her son to return to an empty house.

It had been difficult for her to assuage the guilt she had felt at first, going to work, but Heather had chided her for it.

'Charlie can always come to us for a couple of hours if necessary,' she had told her. 'You know that. You need this job, Win—not just for the money. You need it for yourself. You've devoted yourself exclusively to Charlie when he's needed you most. Just remember, another handful of years and he'll be gone.'

Even though she had acknowledged the truth of Heather's comments and even though she felt that both Charlie and herself had benefited from the independence her job gave them both, Win still had these sharp attacks of guilt.

She could hear the television as she walked into the hall. The sitting-room door was open, and through it she could hear Charlie yelling excitedly.

'That's it! Did you see it, Dad? Did you see the way he kicked that goal?

Dad!

Win froze, her nerve-endings screaming a rejection of all that that one simple word conveyed.

'He certainly has some real power there.'

She hadn't heard him speak in over ten years, but she would have recognised his voice in a hundred...in a thousand. Deep, reflective, the words measured and firm, no trace of any

Australian accent, the same voice which had once slurred like honey with desire when he had told her how much he wanted her, how much he loved her. The same voice which had been raw with need when he'd leaned over her in the dark, entering her body.

The same voice which had been hard and cold when he'd condemned her for conceiving their child.

Forcing down the feeling of icy shock threatening her, Win took a deep breath and then, straightening her shoulders, she pushed open the sitting-room door and walked in.

CHAPTER THREE

WIN had learned her lessons and knew now how vitally important it was to seize control and hold on to it.

Without looking at Charlie, she demanded icily, 'What are you doing here, James?'

Out of the corner of her eye, she saw the way Charlie had flushed, how anxious and distressed he looked, but she forced herself to ignore him, instead focusing all her attention on the man who was uncurling himself from the settee and standing up in front of her.

She would have preferred him to remain seated, she acknowledged, just about managing not to give in to the instinctive desire to step back a little from him. *That* betraying piece of body language would mean her giving far more away to him than a couple of feet of floor space. So instead she stood her ground, angling her head so that she could look directly at him, her eyes flashing, her mouth indenting with the hostility she made no attempt to conceal.

She could see the way James looked briefly at Charlie, and her hostility increased. How dared he try to use their son as a pawn between them? How dared he be here in her home in the first place? Why had he come here? He could not have known she wouldn't be here. Unless . . .

Win stiffened immediately and only just resisted the desire to turn round and look fully at Charlie. What she had interpreted as confusion could just as easily have been guilt.

Had Charlie lied to her about his arrangements for the afternoon? Had he known—arranged with James that he would come round? she wondered in disbelief.

Before James could say anything, Charlie had come to stand beside her.

'I said he could come here,' he told her. 'After all, it's my home too, and he *is* my father.' His chin jutted out as he spoke, and helplessly Win recognised that, for all his bravado, he was very close to tears. She forced back her own shock, habit enabling her to control and dismiss her own emotions.

Later, she would have to point out to him that, his home or not, it was still wrong for him to have done what he had, but she couldn't humiliate him by doing so in front of James, so she simply said quietly, 'Yes, it *is* your home as well, Charlie.'

As she looked away from him, she realised that James was studying her with a frown. Probably wondering what on earth he had ever seen in her, she reflected acidly. She certainly wasn't in the same class as the Taras of this world. She wondered what had happened to the other woman.

James had never remarried, and if there was a woman in his life he hadn't introduced her to Charlie while their son had been staying with him.

'I'm sorry,' James apologised briefly. 'I had no idea you weren't aware that I was coming.'

'I knew you were returning to the area,' she countered coolly, 'but no, I did *not* expect to come home and find you sitting in *my* living-room.'

She stressed the 'my', and was pleased to see the faint darkening of colour touching his cheekbones. So he wasn't totally impervious to his own guilt in taking advantage of an offer he must have known she would never have countenanced. Good.

'Well, we won't delay you,' she continued smoothly. 'I'm sure you've got things to do.'

She tensed as she saw the look that passed between father and son, and felt the tiny hairs standing up on the back of her neck.

'Dad's moving in here with us,' Charlie informed her, then added rebelliously, '*I* told him it was all right.'

For a moment Win thought she might actually faint. This time Charlie had quite definitely gone too far.

Above the painful buzzing in her head and ears, she heard James saying, 'I'm sorry, I thought you knew. In fact...' He stopped speaking abruptly while Win stared at her son in angry disbelief.

Charlie knew quite well that the last thing she would want was to have James living under their roof, and for him to have implied anything different to his father had to have been a deliberate deception.

But if she was angry with Charlie, it was nothing to the bitterness and fury she felt for James. He surely must have known that Charlie was lying to him in implying that she would ever countenance letting him step over her front door, never mind move in.

Yes, of course he had known it. He was far too intelligent not to have done so.

'If this is some kind of joke, James——' she began icily, having taken a steadying breath.

'Not as far as I'm concerned,' James informed her.

'Well, it must be quite obvious that you can't stay here.'

'Why can't he?'

Win turned to stare at Charlie.

'Charlie, you know why he can't. We're divorced. He... I...'

'Well, just because *you* want to marry someone else, it doesn't mean that *he's* going to be my father.'

Win felt her heart drop with shock and despair. She hadn't even broached the subject of Tom yet with Charlie. She had honestly believed he had no idea that Tom wanted to marry her, and yet here he was virtually accusing her of

trying to force an unwanted stepfather on him—
and in front of James of all people as well.

'I want *Dad* to live here with *me*,' Charlie
persisted stubbornly. 'After all, it's my house
too,' he repeated.

'And mine.'

The soft words, murmured so that only she
could hear them, stunned Win. She turned her
head slowly away from her son to look at her ex-
husband. Her heart was racing frantically with
shock. What was James trying to say to her?
What kind of *threat* was he trying to make?
Surely he couldn't actually want to move in here
with her? Or was that it? Was he hoping to subtly
force her to move out, leaving him with Charlie?

If her heart had been racing before, it was
nothing to the frantic way it thudded now.

Was that what this was all about? A subtle ploy
not so much to reinforce James's right to half of
her house, but a determined and carefully cal-
culated scheme to drive a wedge between Charlie
and herself and to force her into a position where
she inadvertently allowed her dislike of him to
push her into allowing him to push her out of
their son's life? Because if she moved out of the
house and into a room at the hotel, which she
could quite easily do, that was what would
happen.

Her relationship with Charlie was going
through a very sticky patch. At the moment the
person he wanted in his life was his father—

whether to punish her because he resented her relationship with Tom, or perhaps more simply because he was at an age where he needed to be able to relate more closely to James, she didn't know. The reason didn't really matter—not at this stage. What did matter was that she must not allow her emotions to trap her into doing something she would later bitterly regret.

'I can't really believe you'd want to stay here, James,' she said with a calm she was very far from feeling.

'No? My son *lives* here,' James pointed out to her. 'And since it is so that I can spend more time with him that I've decided to come back...'

Win had to cling to the back of the chair to support herself. She could feel her whole body starting to tremble, and to her horror she discovered she was perilously close to doing something she hadn't done in nearly a decade. She was about to cry.

Well, not here she wasn't. Not in front of this man. Taking a deep breath, she gave him a tight-lipped condemnatory look.

'Don't think I haven't realised what you're up to, James,' she told him quietly. 'But you're not going to win, you know.'

She gave a brief look at Charlie and, summoning a taut smile, told him, 'Well, Charlie, since it appears that we're going to have a house guest, you'd better take your father upstairs and show him the spare room.'

'I already know it. It's the room which used to be ours, I believe. I used to live here, remember?' James taunted her. 'And besides...' He too looked down at Charlie. 'Charlie and I have already taken my stuff up there, haven't we, old son?'

Win had to turn away from him in case her face betrayed her.

'Mum, I'm hungry,' Charlie announced plaintively.

Despairingly, Win wondered how on earth she was supposed to block out the shock of suddenly discovering that her ex-husband was not only here in her house, but that he had moved in and intended to make it his home; to concentrate on the ordinary mundane task of preparing and cooking a meal.

All she really wanted to do was crawl away somewhere dark and safe, curl into a small foetal ball and allow the physical effects of her shock to take over her body, but even that release was denied her now, she admitted bitterly. She couldn't even shut herself away in her bedroom for half an hour without Charlie questioning what she was doing, and no doubt James guessing just how fragile her control over herself was.

Oh, he definitely had the upper hand over her. How long had he been plotting this...manoeuvring Charlie, teaching him to go behind her back, to deceive and lie to her?

That was what hurt her most of all, she acknowledged painfully. The fact that Charlie's hero-worship of his father had totally destroyed the trust and loyalty she had believed the two of them had shared. Charlie had known she would never have agreed to having James live here with them.

Instinctively her anger focused not on Charlie, her child, but on his father. Charlie was only a child still, albeit one who was old enough to know that what he had done was wrong, but James was an adult, and in conspiring with their child so that Charlie would behave so deceitfully, by blatantly encouraging him to lie to her, James had totally ignored his responsibilities as a father and as an adult.

How on earth was Charlie supposed to accept and appreciate the importance of being honest when his own father was teaching him deceit?

She could feel the heavy miasma of despair and hurt descending over her. She had tried so hard to instil into Charlie the kind of values she believed were important. It hadn't always been easy; Charlie had more than his fair share of rebellious male pride and did not always welcome Win's strict code of ethics, especially now that he was getting older, and it had caused her several moments of disquiet recently to see how much he preferred to follow the example of his peers, rather than to listen to her.

When she had discussed this with Heather, Heather had counselled her not to be too upset.

'Danny's just the same,' she had comforted her. 'It's always, "Well, everyone else does, or everyone else has..." I think it's a kind of kids' mafia they operate.'

'You don't think, then, that it's because Charlie doesn't have a father?' Win had asked Heather uncertainly, confessing hesitantly, 'Everything I do these days seems wrong, Heather. He'd rather listen to his male teachers at school than to me, and I hate the way he suddenly seems to regard everyone female with—well, almost contempt. I keep asking myself if I've done that to him, if somehow I've given him the idea that women are second class in some way.'

'I know what you mean,' Heather had told her. 'Danny's just the same at the moment. I actually caught him telling Jenny last week that he wasn't going to help her with the washing up any more because it's women's work. I don't know where they pick it up from—it seems to be an instinctive male thing. Hopefully it's just a phase and they'll grow out of it. If not,' she promised darkly, 'Danny will probably get it stamped out of him, by Jenny if not by me.'

Dutifully Win had laughed, trying to accept her friend's reassurance that Charlie was simply growing up and beginning to test his masculinity.

'I know it's hard,' Heather had told her as she left. 'One moment they're all cuddles and kisses—and somehow little boys *are* much more loving and dependent than little girls—and then the next they're treating you as though you're the lowest form of life. Believe me, Win, it isn't anything you have or haven't done. Mind you, I have had to point out to Rick that it would help matters if Danny saw him doing a bit more around the house.'

Which had only reinforced her greatest fear, Win reflected now. Was she guilty of depriving Charlie of a very necessary male presence in his life? Was she the one who was really to blame for him turning away from her?

She had tried her best. Heather had helped, always making sure that Charlie was included in their family outings so that he didn't suffer the isolation often experienced by only children.

Of course, if her brothers and their families had lived closer, it would have helped, but they were scattered all over the world now, and Win's finances were such that visits to see them were out of the question.

Once, years ago, when she had been desperately in need of a new winter coat, Heather had protested that if she had bought Charlie less expensive clothes she could have afforded to buy something decent for herself. Win had told her friend quietly that Charlie's clothes came out of the money sent to her by his father and that it was a matter of pride with her never to touch a penny of that money for anything for herself.

What wasn't spent on things that Charlie needed was banked in a building society account in his name.

'Will you be eating with us?' she asked James frigidly, immediately mentally berating herself. She ought to have simply ignored him, to have frozen him out of the intimacy of her life with Charlie, instead of stupidly making it even easier for him to infiltrate himself into it.

She wasn't in the least deceived. A man of James's wealth and standing could hardly really want to live in such homely surroundings. He was probably more used to the luxury of a private hotel suite, with constant room service, his every whim attended to, she decided sourly. Well, it wasn't going to be like that here.

So why had she so stupidly asked if he wanted to share their meal?

Trying to recoup the ground she had so carelessly thrown away, she added quickly, 'I expect you'd prefer to eat out. Charlie and I only have very simple meals, and this evening's will be something cold, as I'm going out later.'

'Really? Then perhaps it would be better if I took Charlie off your hands and the two of us went out somewhere?'

'No!'

Her colour high, Win knew that her denial had been too quick and too forceful.

'No, that won't be necessary,' she told James more quietly.

He was looking directly at her, and she was too proud to look away. She could see the cool assessment in his eyes and knew instinctively that he was looking for her vulnerabilities, her weaknesses, that he was stalking her, hunting her, hoping to panic her into giving in.

She returned his scrutiny, her own eyes guarded and wary, reluctantly acknowledging that in putting her on the defensive he had already won too much ground from her.

All right, so he had had the advantage of surprise, she told herself as she walked into the kitchen, but the war wasn't over yet, and he would soon discover that there was no way she was going to allow him to take Charlie away from her.

But could she stop him taking Charlie's love from her?

Her hand trembled on the handle of the fridge door, tears smarting painfully at the back of her eyes. Fiercely she blinked them away. That was *all* she needed—to start crying. She hadn't cried since...since Charlie fell off his bike when he was five years old and had suffered a mild dose of concussion.

She had felt so alone then, afraid. Her parents had retired to Edinburgh where her mother had grown up, her brothers and their families were all living overseas, and Heather and her family had been away on holiday. There had been no one with whom she could share her fear, or her guilt.

Charlie had recovered, of course. The concussion had only been very mild. Since then he had broken his arm, sprained his wrist and suffered all the normal injuries of an active growing boy, but that had been the last time she had given in to the drowning panic and self-pity of longing for someone of her own to turn to, someone of her own to share her burdens and worries, someone of her own to love her.

Since then she had taught herself that if she had no one to love her then she had no one to hurt her either. And James had hurt her—so badly, in fact, that sometimes in her darkest moments she wondered if she had ever truly recovered from the pain of discovering he no longer loved her.

Some women were like that, attracting the wrong kind of man, loving a man who would ultimately only cause them pain. That was why she was being so cautious about committing herself to Tom—or at least it was one of the reasons.

The antagonism which existed between Tom and Charlie was of course another. And the lack of excitement sexually. Her hand trembled again as she reached for the fridge.

No, that was not an important issue, she told herself firmly. In fact, if she was honest, the last thing she wanted at this time in her life was to re-experience all the tumultuous, dangerous, un-controllable emotions and sensations she had experienced sexually with James.

'Anything I can do to help?'

The quiet offer made her body jerk violently in shock. She hadn't heard James walk into the kitchen, but now she was acutely conscious of him standing immediately behind her. It was as though his body were giving off an intense heat which somehow reached out to surround and engulf her own, sending up her pulse-rate, over-heating her skin, so that it was excruciatingly over-sensitive to his physical presence behind her.

'No, thanks, I can manage,' she told him shortly. The kitchen was only a small room and she didn't want him in it with her. It made her feel short of breath, her body taut with a curious aching tension almost like the onset of a particularly virulent type of flu.

'Doesn't Charlie help you with this?' James asked her, gesturing towards the table she was in the process of laying.

Thankful that she had her back to him, Win was nevertheless all too conscious of the tide of defensive colour sweeping up over her body. She knew she had not imagined the censure in his voice, the suggestion that somehow she was not bringing Charlie up properly.

'Charlie does his fair share of chores,' she told him angrily. What she did not want to admit to him was that lately—she suspected as a show of

defiance and resentment of her relationship with
Tom—Charlie had slowly stopped helping her to
prepare their meals as he had once done. He had
also become irritatingly untidy, and she bit her
lip, remembering the row they had had the previous weekend, when he had refused to make his
bed.

To her relief Win heard Charlie call out from
the sitting-room.

'Dad... Dad, come and watch this.'

As she turned away, her scalp prickled with
her awareness of James still standing behind her.
Why was he hesitating? That was why he was
here, wasn't it? To inveigle his way into Charlie's
heart and to displace her from their son's life?

'Charlie wants you,' she told him unnecessarily.

'Yes,' she heard him agree, 'he does.'

And as she heard the note of triumph in his
voice she wished she had not allowed herself to
give in to the temptation to make that small acid
remark. The gulf of experience and maturity
which had once yawned so widely between herself
and James no longer existed, and it certainly
wasn't necessary for her to feel as though she had
anything to prove to him.

Except that Charlie's place was with her.

Despite her torturous thoughts, her hands
moved deftly, preparing the meal. The Win who
had once barely known how to boil an egg or
iron a shirt had given way to the capable woman
she was now, years ago. The cold chicken they

were having had been basted in a light grape sauce which she knew Charlie loved; the mixture of salad and raw vegetables she was serving with it showed an expert knowledge of nutrition and just what was most likely to appeal to a young appetite. The rolls in the basket were healthy wholegrain; she and Charlie ate them without any kind of spread or butter, and, while she ordered skimmed milk for herself, for Charlie she ordered the full cream variety to ensure that he got the proper amount of nutrition.

She was lucky in that at least—Charlie had never been a faddy eater.

They were having strawberries for 'afters' with Charlie's favourite ice-cream. Win made it herself in bulk and froze it, and now, as she scooped some out of the container to put in a bowl in the fridge, she called, 'It's ready, Charlie. Upstairs, please, to wash your hands.'

Silence.

She closed the fridge door and walked into the sitting-room. Charlie was lying on the floor with his head propped up on his hands, his favourite television-watching position.

'Charlie, I said tea's ready.'

'I just want to watch this,' Charlie told her.

Win glanced at the screen. She was almost sure that the programme flickering on the screen was not really of any interest to her son and that he was just being difficult, and where normally she would simply have switched off the set and told him firmly that since he had not told her there was something on which he specifically wanted to watch, and since he had been the one to say he was hungry, he would just have to forgo the rest of the programme, she was hesitant to do so in front of James.

Miserably she recognised that there were going to be far more problems for her to deal with in having James living with them than she had first feared.

In the initial wave of shock and disbelief, all she had been able to think was how was she going to manage to cope with living in close physical proximity to the man who had once been her husband, her lover. Now she was beginning to believe that that would be the least of her worries; that, given her present relationship with Charlie, the last thing she was going to have time for was to worry about her own responses to James's presence.

While she stood in the doorway, hesitating, angry with both herself and with Charlie but most of all bitterly resentful of James for the way he was manipulating them both, James stood up and calmly walked over to the TV set, switching it off.

'Do as your mother says, Charlie,' he commanded quietly.

Win wasn't sure which of them was the more shocked, Charlie or herself.

Certainly she was the one to recover fastest, barely waiting until Charlie, after one incredulous look at his father, had slowly got up and gone upstairs to say fiercely, 'Thank you, James, but I'm perfectly capable of dealing with Charlie without your interference.'

'I'm sure you are,' he agreed blandly—too blandly, Win recognised as she tried to force down the lump of leaden rage lodging in her throat. As he turned away from her and opened the door, he added drily, 'Still, it does seem that Charlie needs a little help in realising it, doesn't it?'

'Where are you going?' she demanded tensely as he walked into the hall.

He paused to look at her, his cool gaze taking in her flushed face and angry eyes.

'Upstairs to wash my hands,' he told her mockingly. 'Isn't that what a good parent should do? Not simply command a child into obedience but show him or her by example?'

As she turned away from him, Win acknowledged that she had allowed him to score another point against her.

How long could she cope with this level of emotional and mental pressure? Already her nerve was going, fraying, threatening to betray her into anger and fear.

*   *   *

Mm, chicken's good.'

Win wasn't eating anything, but now her head jerked upwards as James spoke.

'It's Mum's special recipe,' Charlie informed him.

As she saw the brief look of surprise cross his face, Win wondered if James was remembering the disastrous meals she had once tried to cook for him, and for the first time since his arrival she allowed herself to feel a tiny flicker of hope and triumph. If she could surprise him with something as simple as her cooking, then perhaps there was hope that she could outwit him yet. After all, surely all she had to do was to wait, and then sooner or later he would betray himself to Charlie in his real colours. He was, after all, the same man who had told her angrily that their son should never have been conceived. The same man who had been too busy to be with her when Charlie was born, the same man who had complained about Charlie crying, who had refused to allow him to sleep in their room, who had complained about the mess his presence caused.

She couldn't resist taunting him a little.

'Yes, Charlie and I enjoy trying out new recipes, don't we, Charlie?' Without waiting for him to reply she added, 'I suppose you thought I still hadn't learned how to boil an egg?'

'I hadn't really given the matter much thought,' James told her carelessly, somehow managing to diminish both her and all that she had achieved in the years since their divorce as totally unimportant, and while she was still recovering from that blow Win heard him adding, 'What *did* occur to me was that, as a working mother, you might not have much time for home cooking. I noticed you've got a microwave.'

Win could feel the rage burning through her, raw as acid, and just as destructive. Somehow she just—only just—managed to stop herself from getting up and walking out.

As she forced herself to ignore his comment and to turn away from him to ask Charlie if he still wanted to see a particular video he had mentioned to her, she tried to fight down her growing feeling of fear and panic.

How was it that James constantly managed to outmanoeuvre her like this? She was not a person who lost her temper, her control, easily, and yet within the space of a few hours he had managed to bring her to the point where she could all too easily have done so with just a few carefully chosen barbs.

She must not allow him to get to her like this. She must try to use her intelligence and her intellect to distance herself a little from what was happening. She must not get so emotional, so defensive.

She couldn't eat her pudding, pushing it round and round her dish until finally she pushed it abruptly away.

'Come on, old son, let's you and me do the
washing up,' she heard James suggesting to
Charlie. 'That will give your mother a chance to
get ready for her date.'

The phone rang abruptly, causing Win to stare
blindly at it for a second before getting to her
feet and walking tensely over to it.

It was Tom on the other end of the line, ringing
to confirm the time he was picking her up for
their date.

'No, I hadn't forgotten,' she assured him, her
mouth dry, her back stiff with the tension of the
silence from the table behind her. 'Yes, I'll be
ready at eight,' she agreed.

As she replaced the receiver, then turned
round, she saw that Charlie was scowling at her,
and her heart sank.

'That was Tom,' she told him unnecessarily.
'He...we're going out tonight.'

As she spoke she realised she would have to
ring Heather to cancel the arrangement she had
made for Charlie to sleep over with Danny. That
wouldn't be necessary, not now that he had his
precious, wonderful father here with him.

Feeling more exhausted and miserable than she
could remember feeling since the early days after
the divorce, she walked towards the door, all too
aware both of Charlie's truculent resentment that
she was going out, and James's impassive
scrutiny.

CHAPTER FOUR

Win was halfway up the stairs when she saw James walking into the hall below her. He was on his own, and he closed the sitting-room door firmly behind him, staring up at her, his face hard and set as he demanded,

'Tell me something, Win. Do you make a habit of leaving Charlie on his own so that you can see your lover?'

The attack was so unexpected, so unjustified, that for a moment Win simply could not think of a single thing to say. Her colour came and went, while her heart thundered in angry, fearful protest at his accusation. Her head ached, and when she put a hand up to her temple she discovered that her hand was trembling as violently as though she had developed some physical weakness.

'I *never* leave Charlie on his own,' she told him huskily, her voice low and strained.

'You did this afternoon,' James pointed out.

Her head was spinning, her thoughts and emotions in chaos.

'He was supposed to be with friends.' What was she doing, letting James force her into this defensive position? Why didn't she simply tell

him that, if he had not taught Charlie to deceive
her, Charlie would not have been on his own.

'I've arranged for him to stay overnight with
a friend tonight,' she added, knowing that it was
too late to go back and retrieve the ground she
had just lost.

'Stay overnight?' The dark eyebrows lifted.
'How very convenient—but then, with all those
hotel bedrooms at your disposal, I suppose the
pair of you hardly need to wait until Charlie's
out of the way, do you?'

Win stared down at him in complete disbelief.
This was taking the war into a territory she had
never dreamed he would dare to enter.

'How dare you suggest such a thing?' she
breathed hotly. 'And besides...'

'Besides what?'

'My personal life has absolutely nothing to do
with you,' she told him. She was almost in tears
of anger and shock, that he should have the gall
to introduce so personal a subject with her.

'No, but it has to Charlie,' he told her unre-
pentantly. 'Or don't you care that he doesn't like
your lover, and that he most certainly doesn't
want him as a stepfather?'

She ached with pain to know that Charlie had
discussed her and her relationship with Tom with
James, but there was nothing she could say, no
retaliation she could make to his question other
than to say huskily, 'Of course I care. Charlie's

my son,' she told him fiercely. 'He's the most important person in my life.'

'Is he?' The dark eyebrows rose again, the cool eyes shadowed and watchful. 'Does your lover know that?'

Win turned her back on him and continued on her way upstairs without answering him. What, after all, could she say?

She telephoned Heather from her bedroom, and knew her friend was aware that something was wrong from the tone of her voice, but all she could do was say to her, 'Heather, I can't talk about it right now. Tomorrow, perhaps,' before she replaced the receiver and then curled up on her bed, rocking herself to and fro as the trauma of what was happening engulfed her.

Of course, she couldn't really allow herself the self-indulgence of giving way to her shock. Tom was due at eight, and it was gone seven now. She had to shower and change, wash and dry her hair, put on her make-up and somehow manage to appear calm and in control when she went downstairs to say goodnight to Charlie.

Because she didn't want Charlie to realise what she was really feeling, or because she wanted to keep her feelings hidden from his father?

In the end, she didn't go downstairs until she actually saw Tom's car coming down the lane. Angry with herself for her lack of courage and for allowing James to actually make her feel that she was doing something wrong in seeing Tom, she went into the sitting-room, and Charlie, whom she had heard chatting happily to James, glowered silently at her when she went to give him a brief hug, pulling back from her.

'Don't forget, bed at ten,' she reminded him as evenly as she could, trying not to feel hurt at his rejection of her.

Leaving them both in front of the TV, and trying to tell herself she was being a fool for feeling like an outcast, she headed for the front door. She was just about to open it when she heard James call her name.

Tensely she turned round, storm signals darkening her eyes as she waited for his verbal attack. But instead the floor seemed to rock beneath her feet as he said quietly, 'I know it's hard, Win, but try to understand. In Charlie's eyes you're rejecting him in favour of another man. He's jealous, and it hurts—my God, how it hurts.'

The last few words were muttered almost under his breath, making her heart suddenly tighten as she wondered helplessly about the woman who had taught him that kind of pain, then she was forcing herself to fight down that painful twist of emotion, to summon all her defences and remember just exactly what he was trying to do. 'Thank you,' she told him shakily. 'But I don't need you to explain my son's feelings to me.'

'*Our* son,' James corrected her softly. 'Our son, Win, not just yours.'

Win's heart was beating suffocatingly fast as she walked through the door.

Tom was halfway up the garden path. He frowned when he saw her, asking her, 'What's wrong?'

'Not now,' she told him shortly, shaking her head. She didn't trust herself to start speaking yet. She was too afraid of what she might say.

The restaurant where they were having dinner was a new one. Tom wanted to try it out to see if he could usefully adapt or incorporate part of its menu into his own.

Win knew that the bill for this evening's meal would be set against hotel expenses—Tom was that kind of man. He would not understand if she told him she would rather have eaten somewhere less expensive and for the meal to be strictly personal, instead of being partially business.

Tom lived, breathed, ate and slept the hotel; that was how he had managed to turn it into such a success, and, while she applauded his hard work and drive, sometimes she wished he was a little less ambitious and aggressive.

Wanting to be successful was all very well, but there were other things in life, such as having a family. She frowned as she sat beside him in his car and waited for him to start the engine. If she and Tom married and did have a family, how would that affect Charlie?

'Nice car,' Tom commented, glancing at James's Daimler. 'Looks a bit out of place down here, though,' he added slightly disparagingly, so oblivious to her own angry irritation at the way he categorised what was after all her home. 'Know who owns it?'

'It belongs to Charlie's father,' Win told him quietly.

She had his attention now. His head turned towards her. He was frowning, his glance suddenly intent and sharp.

'I thought he was supposed to be in Australia.'

Was that a note of accusation she could hear in his voice, as though somehow he thought she had lied to him?

Quickly she stifled the thought. The shock of James's arrival and of discovering how Charlie had lied to her had made her over-sensitive and prone to over-react.

'He was,' she agreed. 'However, it seems that he's decided to move back here. He wants to be closer to Charlie.

She closed her eyes as she spoke, willing back the tears she could feel burning the back of her eyes, but she couldn't keep the despair out of her voice.

If she had expected Tom to be sensitive to what she was feeling, she was doomed to disappointment. Instead of picking up on her fear, he was frowning.

'What exactly do you mean, Win? He's decided to move back here? He's not moving back *permanently*, is he?'

Silently Win nodded, trying to speak past the huge lump in her throat. Now that she was away from the house and it was no longer so vital for her to prevent James from seeing how shocked and distressed she was by his presence, she was suddenly sharply aware of just how much of a shock she had actually suffered.

She felt almost as traumatised as she had done when she was first divorced. Then the build-up of pain and despair had been slow and gradual; now...now the shock of actually finding James in her home, of hearing him say that he had been invited there by Charlie, of knowing—not just fearing, but knowing that somehow he intended to take Charlie from her, was suddenly making itself felt physically and emotionally to a devastating extent.

Her eyes kept blurring with tears. She felt sick, cold as ice, her brain somehow almost detached from her body, her emotions see-sawing wildly out of control.

'He wants Charlie, Tom, I know it. He's already driving a wedge between us.' The words spilled from her in sharp bursts raw with pain and fear. 'And now, with him actually living with us——'

'Living with you?' Tom cursed as he took his eyes off the road, braking sharply. 'What the hell do you mean?'

Win looked back at him.

'Exactly what I said. When I got back from work this afternoon, I found that *Charlie* had invited his father to move in with us.'

She didn't like the way Tom was looking at her.

'And *you* let him. For God's sake, Win, I've tried to warn you before about the trouble you're storing up for yourself by letting that brat of yours rule your life.'

'Charlie is *not* a brat.'

Tom glared at her.

'Not in your eyes,' he agreed. 'Look, don't tell me you're simply going to sit back and let the guy stay? God, Win, what the hell are people going to think when you've got your ex moving back in with you playing at happy families, when people know that you and I——?'

'It isn't like that,' Win protested fiercely.

'Then tell him to leave.'

'I can't,' she admitted miserably. 'For one thing, he actually still owns half the house, and for another...' She looked out of the window, blinking away her tears and biting her bottom lip. 'Tom, I'm afraid that if I do then Charlie will leave with him. Legally I have full custody, but if Charlie chooses to be with his father...'

She heard Tom curse again as he set the car in motion.

'Do you know what *I* think?' he demanded savagely. '*I* think the best thing that could happen, for us anyway, would be for the kid to go to his father. Hell, Win, you know that he and I don't get on. And no offence, but—well, the last thing I want when we're married is to have a sullen, jealous adolescent coming between us. One day we'll have kids of our own, and I'm not sure I'd want to take the risk of ever leaving him alone with them.'

'Tom, that's completely unfair.' Win was horrified by what he was suggesting, her face white with distress as she looked at him.

'Sorry, but that's the way I see it,' he told her, shrugging aside her distress. 'Basically the kid's too damn possessive about you, Win.'

'That's not true,' she protested.

Of course the evening wasn't a success. Tom was awkward and aggressive with the restaurant staff, making Win feel uncomfortably self-conscious. She was still smarting from his remarks about Charlie, and by the time they actually left the restaurant she was admitting painfully that it had shocked her to discover just how insensitive he was to her unhappiness and fear over her son.

A tiny voice inside her asked her sharply if this was actually the sort of man she wanted to marry; someone so insensitive to her fears and needs that he carelessly dismissed them. And as for his criticisms of Charlie... She closed her eyes, visualising a life in which she was constantly having to appease either one or the other of the males in her life.

By the end of the evening she was so emotionally exhausted that even Tom's peevish sulkiness failed to trigger her into wanting to make any kind of guilty reparation for having caused it.

When he stopped the car outside her house she reached immediately for the door-handle.

'Can't wait to get back to them, can you?' Tom accused sourly. 'Good in bed, was he, Win?'

Her face flamed with embarrassment and indignation. That was the second time in one evening that a man had asked a too personal question about her sex life.

'I'm sorry if I've spoiled your evening, Tom,' she said tiredly, giving in to the pressure he was putting on her, knowing really that what she felt was not guilt but irritation. Was it really necessary for Tom to behave so childishly, so—so selfishly? Were all males like that—thinking only of themselves? And if so, why? Was it an inherent trait, or was it one that was fostered during their formative years by over-loving mothers?

'Well, I suppose it wasn't your fault,' Tom conceded. She stiffened as unexpectedly he reached for her, pushing her back against the seat as he kissed her.

She tried to tell herself that she enjoyed it, that it was simply foolish at her age to expect to feel that sharp thrill of excitement she had experienced as a girl, to miss the fine tremble of her body, the aching pulse of sweet need she had known when James had kissed her.

That had been years ago, when half the thrill of being kissed by James had come from her own intensity, her own adolescent belief that she was in love—more than half, probably. If James kissed her now she would probably feel exactly as she was doing with Tom, aware of the discomfort of her position, the smell of food on his breath, the anxiety of one of her neighbours walking past the car and seeing them, and the even sharper awareness that the movement of his mouth against hers was doing very little more than making her feel extremely guilty that she found the whole thing so totally unexciting.

Amazingly, he seemed totally oblivious to her lack of response, smiling at her in satisfaction in the darkness as he released her.

'There!' he exclaimed, grinning at her. 'That should have shown that ex-husband of yours just exactly how the land lies.'

Win's heart thumped frantically. What did he mean? Had James been watching them? She glanced towards the house, and saw to her relief that the sitting-room curtains were drawn.

'You *have* told him about us, haven't you?' Tom questioned her.

'*Charlie* has told him,' Win informed him as she opened the car door.

Suddenly she wasn't just unsure about whether she actually loved Tom enough to marry him, she was also unsure if she even liked him any more.

Tiredly she got out of the car, critically noting the way he drove off without even seeing if she got safely inside, never mind escorting her to the door. Tom was like that, though, abrupt, impatient, reluctant to waste time on anything he thought unnecessary.

She remembered when they had made love. Immediately afterwards he had left her to shower, instead of staying with her, holding her.

James had always held her after loving her... held her, touched her, stroked and gently kissed her so that very, very often she eagerly wanted him again.

Her face flushed by the illicit thoughts conjured up by her memory, she unlocked her front door and hurried inside.

The house was totally quiet. Frowning, she glanced at her watch. She wasn't that late; it was only just gone twelve.

She pushed open the sitting-room door. The television screen flickered, but the sound had been turned low. Her heart thumped, then turned over painfully as she saw James lying sprawled fast asleep on the settee. It was really too small for him, and she suspected that when he eventually woke up he would have a stiff neck.

Asleep he looked so much less austere, and far too much like the man she had once loved. His hair fell across his forehead, exactly the same way as Charlie's did, and to her horror she only just managed to stop herself from pushing it back and kissing him lightly as she did to Charlie while he slept.

She was, she realised, numbly, standing far too close to him. How had she got here? She had no memory of walking here from the doorway, but obviously she must have done so. Where his shirt had pulled free of his jeans, she could see a tanned band of firm flesh. Did he still have that same mole on his side?

Her hand was almost touching him when she realised what she was doing. Her breath froze in her lungs, her glance swivelling towards his face in case he was awake and watching her, but to her relief he was still asleep.

As she took a step back from him, she asked herself sickly just what on earth she had thought she was doing.

Had she actually intended to touch him, to push his shirt out of the way, and...? She shivered violently as she took another step backwards, then cried out sharply in alarm as she stumbled on Charlie's discarded trainers, only just managing to stop herself from falling by reaching for the arm of the settee.

James woke immediately, frowning as he sat up, swinging his feet to the floor and reaching out to grab her in one smooth automatic movement that took her completely off guard.

The sensation of his hands on her body, his fingers warm and firm against her flesh, the heat and bulk of his body with its shocking, familiar scent coming so soon after her remembering how it had felt to be held by him, to be kissed by him, overwhelmed logic and reality. For one brief instant she was transported back to the past, her body young and yearning, excited by the proximity of his and all that that proximity promised.

It took his sleep-rough voice demanding huskily, 'Are you OK?' to bring her back to reality. Quickly she pulled back from him, fighting to deny what she had felt, snapping angrily at him.

'Charlie knows he's not supposed to leave his trainers down here.'

'Sorry, they're not Charlie's, they're mine,' James apologised. 'I just meant to relax for a couple of minutes.' He flexed his back as she stepped back from him. 'What's wrong?' he taunted, watching her. 'Disappointed because you didn't get to spend the night with him, is that it?'

Angrily she wheeled away from him and headed for the door, making a detour on her way to her own room to look in on Charlie first.

He was fast asleep. Smiling tenderly, Win bent over him and kissed him. She loved him so much. Too much. Was that possible?

Tiredly she went into her own room.

Three hours later, her body exhausted, but mentally so alert that it was impossible for her to sleep, her muscles ached with the tension caused by her thoughts.

Had she really tonight in Tom's arms actually compared him to James? *Why*? She had never done that before. Why tonight of all nights did she have to recall just how it had felt when James had held her, when James kissed her?

Seeing him again should have reinforced for her all the reasons why their marriage had been destroyed, not made her feel this sick, aching yearning for a sexual intimacy she had long ago come to believe had been more a creation of her own imagination than actual reality.

And yet tonight when he had touched her... She shuddered, clenching her muscles as she fought off the insidious memories of pleasure.

It had not really been like that, she told herself helplessly. She had just convinced herself that it was. What she was remembering were her own daydreams, that was all. And even if there *had* been that pleasure, had it ever been worth the pain which had followed it? Could any amount of physical pleasure be worth that kind of emotional pain?

And besides, what she ought to be concentrating on right now was not the past and whether or not James had actually been the wonderful lover her body remembered, but how on earth she was going to deal with the present, and the threat that James posed to her relationship with Charlie.

Did she have the stamina and the strength of will, the self-control, to stick things out long enough for Charlie to see his father as he actually was? Because she was convinced that ultimately James would show his real colours to Charlie just as he had once done to her.

A small voice whispered treacherously to her that she could always aid the process by telling Charlie the truth, by letting him know that his father had never even wanted him to be born, but she ignored it. She could not do that. The last thing she really wanted was for her son to be hurt. And yet she feared that that was exactly what was going to happen.

CHAPTER FIVE

THE sound of her bedroom door opening woke Win from the deep sleep she had fallen into just before dawn. Her head ached and her eyes felt sore, her eyelids sticking gummily together, evidence of the tears she had wept in the long dark hours when she could no longer keep her fear and despair under control.

Although she had worked the previous day, her normal arrangement with Tom was that she had weekends off so that she could be with Charlie, and part of their weekend routine was for Charlie to cycle down to the paper shop to collect the Sunday papers while she made them their special Sunday breakfast with Charlie's favourite scrambled eggs and the locally made butcher's sausages which he loved.

Now, as she struggled to sit up in bed, quickly finding a tissue to blow her nose and to surreptitiously clean her eyes, she was dismayed to see how late it was—almost gone nine o'clock.

'Hi, Mum. Dad said he'd make breakfast and to let you sleep in. I've brought you some coffee.'

Half a dozen sensations gripped her, none of them happy ones; the first and sharpest was that somehow yet again James had usurped her role in Charlie's life, and that he had cleverly banished her to a minor part, the second resentment and—yes, even jealousy at having the routine she and Charlie had built up between them demolished by James's arbitrarily taking over.

Now as she sat up she could smell the rich aroma of the coffee Charlie was carefully carrying towards her. James had obviously found her cherished small hoard of coffee beans and the grinder.

Her heart turned over, shocking her with the pain that filled her as she took the mug from Charlie and saw that, by some trick of memory, James had made her coffee for her the special way he had made it when they were first married, even to the extent of sprinkling a fine dusting of chocolate on the top.

Who would have thought that such a small careless gesture, a gesture made no doubt to impress Charlie and certainly not made to impress her, should cause her so much pain?

It frightened her to realise how vulnerable she had already become, how afraid and insecure.

'Dad bought the chocolate specially when we went for the papers,' Charlie told her importantly. 'He said you always used to like your coffee like that.'

'Ah, so you *are* awake. I think Charlie was a bit concerned when you didn't wake up at your normal time. I explained to him that sometimes going out on heavy dates could have that effect.'

Win was still holding the coffee-mug, and now some of the liquid splashed down on to her skin as she jumped in shock at the sight of James standing in the open doorway.

Bitterly she looked at him over Charlie's head. How on earth was she going to cope with this continual barrage of destructive barbs, each and every one of them designed to weaken her relationship with her son?

How clever he was, how cruelly aware of her weak points. How long had he been planning this campaign? He had everything on his side, didn't he? she admitted despairingly. The advantage of surprise, the allure of being the absent and therefore more attractive parent, even the fact that he was a man.

She had hardly slept last night through worrying about the future, and she knew her anxiety must show on her tired, make-upless face, while James in contrast looked completely relaxed, virile and very masculinely healthy and alert, his skin tanned from his years in Australia, his hair gleaming, the short-sleeved shirt he was wearing revealing the hard muscles of his arms. Whatever his life had been like in Australia, it had obviously included a good deal of outdoor physical activity. Those muscles, that taut, lean fitness that was so evident in the way he moved, had not come from spending all his time working on computer software programs.

In all the years they had been apart, Win had never questioned how he spent his life, what he was doing and with whom—after all, why should she? He meant nothing to her now. They were divorced—and yet suddenly she had a very clear mental image of him, casually dressed in shorts, adjusting the sails of some small brightly painted boat, while at his side stood a slender, lissom young blonde, her mouth curving in a smile of appreciation as she watched him.

'Your coffee's getting cold.'

The calm comment jolted her back to reality and to the realisation that James was now inside her room, standing at the foot of her bed, sitting down on the edge of it, as casually as though he had every right to that kind of intimacy with her.

Thank heavens she was wearing something! It had been James who had taught her to sleep naked, and in those days, in those first heady days of their marriage, she had had the warmth and sensuality of his body wrapped around her to protect her. After he had gone, she had continued to sleep nude until she realised that part of the reason she was doing so was the insane and hopeless subconscious belief that she might somehow absorb from the bedclothes, the scent of his skin, the warmth of his body, the image of his actual physical presence in what had once been their shared bed. That had been when she had moved out of their room and into this one.

Now, of course, there was Charlie to consider as well. He himself had recently become much more demanding of his own privacy, and she respected his need for that.

The cotton nightshirt she was wearing was serviceable and hardwearing; she had several of them in a variety of colours, and as Charlie mimicked his father and sat on the edge of the bed watching her she reflected sardonically to herself that she doubted the women who had shared James's life over the years had worn such dull things in bed as plain cotton nightshirts—if indeed they *had* worn anything.

Remembering the pleasure of waking to feel James's hands stroking sensuously over her skin, she doubted that they would have, and then immediately she tensed. What on earth was she doing, allowing her senses to conjure up those kind of memories? What she should be remembering was the way James had rejected Charlie, the way he had hurt her, the way he had been unfaithful to her, not how her stupid traitorous body had ached and pulsed for him so long after he had gone that it had been years before she had stopped waking in the night crying out in anguish as she realised that he was not really there.

'Aren't you going to drink your coffee?'

Win stared at the mug she had put down, knowing she could not trust herself to pick it up without her hands trembling betrayingly.

'I drink it black these days,' she told him
coldly. It was the truth, but that didn't mean that
sometimes as a rare treat she didn't allow herself
the luxury of coffee with milk—but never with
that topping of chocolate, which had been something that James had always done for her.

As she moved her head, she saw the disappointment in Charlie's eyes and quickly amended
her statement, remembering that it had been
Charlie who had brought the coffee upstairs to
her.

'Well, perhaps just this once.' She smiled at
Charlie, ignoring James as she picked up the mug
and took a sip.

'Very restrained,' she heard James saying
mockingly. 'I remember a time when you drank
it so enthusiastically that it invariably left a
chocolate rim, just here.'

Win felt her stomach muscles contract while
her brain overloaded on disbelief as he reached
out and lightly traced a line just above her upper
lip. Her furious protest died in her throat, a sensation of dizzying shock flooding her.

She could remember that time too, and she
could remember as well how James had licked
away that soft rim of chocolate, how he had
nibbled teasing little kisses along the whole line
of her mouth, how his teeth had tugged sensuously on her bottom lip until she had cried out
to him in arousal, a small keening sound which

he had taken into his own mouth as he kissed her.

'Dad's taking me out this morning,' Charlie told her, breaking into her dazed awareness that her heart was beating far too fast and that the memories flooding her were not the ones she should be allowing to surface. 'We're going to look for somewhere for him to work.'

'I want to check out the area, study various industrial sites,' she heard James explaining calmly. 'I thought Charlie might like to come with me. Give you some time on your own.'

Win opened her mouth to tell him that she didn't want any time on her own, that Sundays were her and Charlie's special day, but her son was already getting off the bed and walking to the door, calling impatiently, 'Come on, Dad,' and as James turned to follow him she acknowledged miserably that her ex-husband had once again stolen a march on her.

She heard Charlie chattering excitedly to his father as they went downstairs, and a pall of loneliness and misery descended on her. She could always have forbidden Charlie to go out with his father, but she had seen from her son's face how excited he had been, and it was hardly fair of her to deprive him of what he obviously considered to be a treat because of her own jealousy.

Jealousy. Win moved restlessly in her bed. She was jealous of the bond forming between James and Charlie. Jealous and afraid. But she had legal custody of Charlie. But what if James applied to have it overset, or, even worse, if Charlie himself announced that he wanted to live with his father?

In the silence of the now empty house, her feverish imagination worked overtime, visualising a situation where James had re-established himself locally, where he had his own home as well as his business, and where Charlie was becoming increasingly unhappy living with her, perhaps spending weekends with his father, returning full of everything they had done, until one day he announced that he no longer wanted to live with her but with James.

How was she going to cope if that happened? It mustn't happen, she couldn't let it happen. James might want Charlie now—but once he had wanted *her*.

Loving a child was different from loving an adult, she reminded herself—parental love was a word apart from sexual love. But James had not wanted Charlie, she reminded herself stubbornly.

Maybe not then, but he certainly seemed to want him now.

When she got dressed and went downstairs, the kitchen was immaculate, only the whirr of the fan evidence of the meal James and Charlie had eaten. Win was just making herself some coffee when the phone rang. She picked up the receiver, her body tensing a little until she heard Heather's familiar voice.

As briefly as she could, she explained to her friend what had happened, hearing the shocked gasp of breath from the other end of the line.

'You mean he just moved himself in and that's it? You're letting him stay?'

'I haven't got much alternative,' Win told her unhappily. 'Legally he still owns half the house—but it's not just that, Heather, it's Charlie. He dotes on James, and I'm afraid if I make him leave...'

'Oh, Win, I'm so sorry.'

Unlike Tom, Heather sympathised immediately, not needing to have Win's feelings put into words.

'How's Tom taking all this?' Heather asked her cautiously.

Win sighed. 'Not very well.' She paused, and then said painfully, 'He virtually suggested that I just—just hand Charlie over to James like—like an unwanted parcel. I know the two of them haven't exactly hit it off, but I hadn't realised... He was so callous about the whole thing, Heather, and started talking about us having children, him and me, saying he wouldn't relish having Charlie around if we did. I had no idea he felt like that.'

'Well, perhaps it's just as well you found out before you committed yourself to him,' Heather suggested gently.

Win swallowed hard, but she and Heather had known one another too long for any pretence.

'Yes,' she agreed. 'I can't marry him now. I had hoped I could find a way of somehow getting Tom and Charlie to—to come to terms with one another, but now... Charlie's only a boy, Heather,' she burst out painfully. 'I thought Tom would understand, that he'd accept ... that he'd want to do all he could to reassure Charlie that he cared about him. I thought that given time we could be a real family. If our positions had been reversed, if Tom had been the one with a child...'

She heard Heather sigh.

'Men aren't like us, though, are they?' she counselled wryly. 'Some of them can't take any kind of competition or rivalry, sometimes not even when it comes from their own sons, and I'm afraid Tom seems to be that type. I'm so sorry, Win. Look, I could come round if you like.'

'No, no, I'm fine,' Win fibbed, then changed the subject, asking Heather if she intended going to the aerobics class they both attended on Monday evenings.

'Yes, I need it too,' Heather groaned. 'I tried on last year's bikini last night!'

As she replaced the receiver, Win wondered wryly if Tom would ring, then acknowledged that it was highly unlikely. He was not that kind of man, wanting, needing always to have the upper hand. The idea of ringing her to apologise for upsetting her, or even just to reassure her, would be to him tantamount to ceding victory. And yet surely they were supposed to be on the same side?

Perhaps Heather was right, perhaps it *was* as well she had discovered exactly how he felt about Charlie now.

She doubted that there would be any need for her to tell him that she couldn't marry him. He would simply, deftly distance himself from her rather than abruptly ending their personal relationship, she suspected.

She only hoped he would not expect her to give up her job. She had worked so hard for her qualifications *and* her financial independence, and she cherished the feeling of self-worth and self-respect she had gained in doing so.

The girl who had so foolishly ignored the advice of her parents in giving up her individuality to cling adoringly to James had long ago realised her mistake, and the woman who had taken her place now realised how very vitally important it was to her to be treated by others with the respect due to an equal rather than indulged like a child as James had once done.

The silent emptiness of the house disturbed her. Perhaps if she did some cleaning ... It was high time she turned out the small boxroom, and, as she knew from experience, there was nothing like hard physical work for banishing too introspective thoughts.

Half an hour later, hot and out of breath, she sat down ruefully surveying the piles of things she had assembled. How on earth had she managed to accumulate so much rubbish? Her

old school books, for instance. Why had she kept
them? And all these photographs... She frowned
as one of the albums toppled from the pile, dis-
lodging several snaps from inside its covers.

As she bent to pick them up, she recognised
that one of them was of herself. She tensed,
studying it, remembering the day her brother had
taken it, telling her teasingly that when she looked
at it it might remind her to be a little more careful
about becoming accidentally pregnant.

At the time his comment had upset her, but
now, studying it, she could understand his
comment.

Her face, round and slightly swollen, the skin
drawn tight over its puffiness, was the face of a
child, not a woman, her hair tied back in a pony-
tail emphasising the illusion of childishness while
her body, swollen with the baby that would be
Charlie, looked almost grotesque in contrast to
that extreme youthfulness.

Was it merely a trick of the camera that made
her look so young, or had she actually looked
like that? She remembered she had always looked
rather young for her years—after all, at nineteen
she hadn't actually been that young, certainly not
as young as the photograph seemed to suggest.

As she held the snap, her hand started to
tremble. No wonder James had ceased to want
her, she reflected. The wonder was now, looking
at that image of herself, that he had ever wanted
her at all.

With hands that shook she tore the snap in half, pushing the jagged pieces in the middle of a pile of rubbish.

Seeing that old image of herself had hurt her somehow. Because it had justified James's rejection of her?

She didn't need a photograph to remind her how immature she had been; how spoiled and silly in very many ways. But she hadn't been solely to blame. James had encouraged her to fall in love with him, had claimed he loved her in return. But how could he have loved that immature, demanding child? Sometimes when she watched Charlie she was painfully aware that his stubborn wilfulness was something he must have inherited from her, which was perhaps why she was more lenient with him than she should be.

Tiredly she got to her feet, dusting down the knees of her jeans.

When Charlie came home, they could have a bonfire with the rubbish. It was high time she got this room properly sorted out, she decided critically as she put away the things she had decided to keep and stuffed the remainder into plastic bin liners.

Perhaps she could turn it into a small study for Charlie. As she mentally replanned the room, she forced herself to ignore the small voice that mocked that she was making those plans just to keep her fears at bay; that the chances were that any future studying Charlie did would be done not with her, but with his father.

She could feel the anguish burning the back of her throat, a physical reaction to the emotional tumult inside her. Her head still ached, and she lifted her hand to push her hair off her face, grimacing as she saw how dirty it was.

The sunlight glinted on the face of her watch. She looked at it, tensing as she realised how long she had been upstairs. James and Charlie would be back soon and no doubt Charlie would be starving.

Determinedly pushing her fears to the back of her mind, warning herself that to give in to them was to do James's work for him, she carried the full bin liners downstairs and put them outside, before going upstairs to wash and comb her hair.

The jeans she was wearing were old ones, and loose at the waist and on the hips, an indication of the stress she had suffered recently over the antipathy which existed between Tom and Charlie.

Well, at least that was one problem she no longer had to worry about, she acknowledged wearily. She could not marry Tom now, knowing his attitude towards her son.

She touched her face, pinching the skin to give it some colour, dismayed to see how strained and tense she looked. There were some things that not even make-up could conceal, she admitted ten minutes later as she stepped back to inspect the discreet disguise of foundation, eye make-up and lipstick she had applied.

The thick sweater she had pulled on over her jeans disguised the fragility of her body. She wasn't thin—not quite, but if she lost any more weight she would be. Thin and haggard, and distinctly unappealing.

She thought about James, no doubt comparing her with the girls he had known in Australia—young, carefree, voluptuously curved girls, confident of their own powers of attraction, their own sexuality.

She had once felt like that, for a short brilliant sunburst of time in James's arms when he touched her, held her, loved her and told her how much he desired her, how much she delighted him, how much he loved her, and all the ways in which he wanted to pleasure her.

Those at least were promises he *had* kept. Win tensed, putting down her lipstick, her eyes suddenly dark as the forbidden sensations raced through her body. Trapped in the grip of the forces her own reminiscences had set free, she felt her body tremble as she remembered how just the touch of James's hand against her face, just the light brush of his mouth on that deliciously fragile area of flesh where her throat met her shoulder, could bring her whole body achingly alive with desire for him.

She closed her eyes, the lipstick slipping from her fingers as she touched her own breast lightly,

her fingers trembling as she fought to resist the
impulse.

Behind the darkness of her closed eyes, old
images danced and tormented her. James
touching her like that, sliding his hands beneath
her jumper, cupping her breasts while he kissed
her, unfastening her bra, while she shuddered in
pleasure at the sensation of his hands holding her,
his fingers delicate on her nipples, swollen still
from the previous night's passion.

When he removed her jumper she arched up
against him, pulling his head down against her
swollen flesh, rubbing herself against him with
pleading rhythmic urgency, her breath escaping
in a sharp sob as he took her nipple in his mouth
and sucked on it.

Lost in the intensity of her memories, Win was
unaware of the small keening sound she made,
and of the sound of car doors slamming, foot-
steps outside, the front door opening.

'Mum, we're back.'

The sound of her bedroom door opening, and
Charlie's voice announcing their return, shocked
her back to reality. Her eyes snapped open, the
colour rushing to her face, burning her skin as
she saw not only Charlie but James as well.

How long had he been standing there? How
much had he seen . . . realised? The hand that had
been touching her body was now pressed flat to
her side. Beneath the bulkiness of her sweater her
breasts pulsed and ached, her nipples hard and

erect. She could see her reflection in her mirror. Was her arousal as visible to James as it was to her? Had he actually seen, known?

Sick with mortification and embarrassment, she cursed herself for her stupidity. How often in the months, the years after their divorce, when she had comforted herself and the ache in her body with her memories of his lovemaking, had she warned herself that what she was doing was self-destructive?

Charlie was chattering away enthusiastically about what they had seen, and James's Daimler, but Win couldn't concentrate on his conversation. Her face was still flushed, as much with the heat of arousal as with embarrassment, she acknowledged sickly.

'I'm sorry if we disturbed you.'

James's quiet words made her flinch betrayingly, and her head swivelled sharply as she looked at him, guilt and shock mirrored in her eyes, their pupils still visibly dilated.

What did he mean? What was he trying to say? Had he guessed? As she looked away from him, cringing with shame, he came into the room and bent down in front of her. As she focused nervously on him, the sight of his downbent head and his proximity to her body made her stomach ache with sharp physical need. Quickly she stepped back from him.

'You've dropped this,' she heard him saying, and as she forced herself to look at him she saw that he was holding her lipstick. As she felt the slow shaming crawl of colour burn her whole body, she wondered if it was just her guilty conscience that made her think he was looking deliberately and for rather too long at her body, and at her mouth, as though he was subtly telling her that he knew exactly how she had come to drop her lipstick, and even the exact thoughts, the exact memories which had been torturing her when she did.

'Mum, I'm hungry,' she heard Charlie announcing. 'What's for tea?'

She had a piece of lamb which she had originally intended to cook for lunch. It came from the local butcher who supplied and made the sausages. It was Welsh lamb reared in the traditional way, but once they were sitting down to eat it Win found she could barely stand to have it in her mouth. Her stomach was still churning violently from the shame and shock of James walking in on her when she had been so patently, so humiliatingly lost in that wantonly erotic daydream. So much so that she had actually...

She put down her knife and fork. Her breasts still ached, especially the one she herself had so lightly and briefly touched when she was remembering how James—— She pushed away her plate as she felt her gorge rise. How could she have done that, felt that, wanted...?

She stumbled to her feet, knowing James was watching her, but too nauseous to care. In the kitchen she ran the tap, poured herself a glass of cold water and started to sip it when James came in.

'Are you all right?'

'A bit of a headache. It's nothing,' she lied while her throat burned with pain and resentment. How dared he pretend concern when he must know how she felt about having him here—about seeing him with Charlie, about...about everything?

Not even to herself could she admit that what was upsetting her the most was the humiliation of opening her eyes and seeing him standing there, wondering if he had been watching her, if he had seen...

'Some fresh air would probably do you more good than tablets,' she heard him telling her drily.

Her temper snapped. She put down the glass and whirled round, her eyes blazing.

'You might have inveigled your way in here, James. You might be able to threaten and bully me into letting you stay, you might even be able to convince Charlie that you're Superman and God all rolled into one, but none of that gives you the right to start telling *me* what to do. I'm a woman now, not a child, and——'

'Yes, I know you are.' The soft words silenced her. 'Very much a woman.'

His glance rested on her mouth. Her heartbeat seemed to slow down to a dull unsteady thump that physically shook her body. Her mouth had gone dry, the anger draining from her, leaving her weak and helpless.

James was looking at her body now, the topaz brilliance of his eyes surely much more intense, his slow study of her almost a physical caress. She wanted to cry out to him to stop what he was doing, but her vocal cords were paralysed. If he came towards her now, touched her now...

The kitchen door swung open and Charlie came in.

'What's for pudding?' he asked her.

Dizzily Win focused on him, and heard herself replying unsteadily, 'It's fruit *compote*, Charlie, and there's some yoghurt to go with it if you want it.'

How normal and mundane the words were, how ordinary and domesticated her actions in taking Charlie's empty plate from him and going over to the fridge, but inside her body was still trembling in the after-effect of what had happened, and her voice sounded husky, and disturbed—as disturbed as her body felt.

It was her own fault, she told herself later. If she had not provided James with that shaming, betraying glimpse of her sensual vulnerability, she doubted that it would ever have occurred to him to turn that weakness against her, another weapon in his war to take Charlie from her.

She had no illusions, no doubts at all as to why he was now deliberately trying to torment her.

He wanted to undermine her just as much as he could. He wanted to break her and to destroy her relationship with Charlie, and he didn't care what means he used to do so.

CHAPTER SIX

Two nights virtually without any sleep was definitely two too many, Win reflected tiredly as she got out of bed. Even worse, it was Monday morning, she was due at work at nine, and first she had to drop Charlie off at school.

She grabbed her robe and headed for the bathroom, hesitating as she opened the bedroom door, but there was no sound from James's room and the door was shut.

After all, there was no reason for *him* to be up early, she told herself wearily as she went into the bathroom and locked the door. She showered quickly, washed her hair and brushed her teeth, dried herself and went into Charlie's room to make sure he was awake before going back to her own bedroom to get dressed.

Then it was downstairs to start on breakfast, while she kept an eye on the time and listened to the news on the radio; a familiar mundane routine, and certainly not one that should cause her heart to thump so heavily nor her body to be so tense.

But then, of course, what was not familiar was having James living here with her... With them.

She frowned as the pips went, and went to the bottom of the stairs to chivvy Charlie.

Her own breakfast was a bowl of fresh fruit salad and some wholemeal toast, plus at least two mugs of black coffee. Charlie's was more substantial—cereal and milk, wholemeal toast and fresh orange juice.

One eye on the clock, she started to prepare Charlie's packed lunch, grimacing a little over his choice of cold wholemeal pizza, adding some home-made fruit biscuits, plus a small carton of fruit salad and some fruit juice. Some days Charlie opted for the school lunch, some days he preferred to take something cold; so far she had not had any problems with him wanting to go into town and eat at one of the fast-food chains. The school were very strict about pupils below the fifth form level leaving school premises during school hours.

When Charlie came down for his breakfast, she went upstairs to dry her hair and do her face. Charlie had left the bathroom door open and she could see the wet towels lying on the floor. Grimly she called back downstairs to him.

'Bathroom, Charlie. You know where the laundry basket is.'

Reflecting that it would have been easier to remove the towels herself, but acknowledging that to do so was to encourage Charlie in the kind of selfish male laziness she did not want him to develop, she firmly ignored the temptation to remove the towels and went back downstairs.

A quick gulp of her coffee. A reminder to Charlie not to forget his sports kit.

'I'll pick you up from Heather's as usual,' she told him, dashing back upstairs to re-clean her teeth and re-apply her lipstick.

James's door was still closed, and she frowned as she walked past it. Should she knock and offer him a cup of coffee? There was plenty in the jug.

Sternly she reminded herself that he was not here as her guest. If he wanted coffee he could make his own.

Brushing her hair, she caught it back with combs, then secured it in her nape with a ribbon. It was a simple style, but both businesslike and yet not too intimidating.

The towels were still on the bathroom floor.

'Charlie!' she called in exasperation.

'All right, all right.'

She was halfway downstairs when the front door opened and James came in. He had quite obviously been running, his hair slick with sweat, the front of his sports shirt openly damp. Win blinked at him as though she had seen an apparition, causing him to stop and focus on her, then look at her a second time, giving her a long lingering inspection that left her burning from top to toe with resentment and the kind of physical awareness that made her heart jerk dangerously.

'Charlie, come *on*!' she called out. 'You know I have to be at the hotel for nine. If you're not ready in two minutes flat you're going to have to walk.'

It was a regular threat, and one she had never put into force, but James frowned as he heard her make it.

'Look, *I* can run him to school,' he told her.

Cursing herself and him, Win was just about to refuse when Charlie suddenly came clattering down the stairs behind her, grinning from ear to ear.

'Could you, Dad? That would be mega! I can't wait for the others to see the Daimler.'

It was her anger against James that made Win snap crossly at Charlie.

'That's a very unpleasant attitude, Charlie. It isn't material possessions that are important. It's what a person is.'

'Yeah, yeah, I know,' Charlie told her grumpily, going past her into the kitchen.

'Isn't it rather early in the day for moral lectures?' James asked her wryly. As she turned angrily away from him, he added quietly, 'Oh, and by the way, Win, just in case that comment was more for my benefit than Charlie's, let's get one thing straight, shall we? Using money or possessions to bribe my way into anyone's affections, but most especially my son's, isn't something I'd ever stoop to.'

Why was it that, no matter what she said or did, he always managed to outmanoeuvre her? Win asked herself miserably ten minutes later as she got into her car with Charlie.

From there the day went from bad to worse.

Tom was obviously in a mood with her, punishing her for what had happened on Saturday by finding fault with the meticulous arrangements she had made for a conference due to begin later in the week.

Patiently Win listened to him, keeping a tight rein on her temper by reminding herself how much she wanted to keep her job. She and Tom already had a policy of keeping things on a strictly business footing at work, so she wasn't surprised that he didn't make any direct reference to Saturday evening, but it did both irritate and upset her that he should make several small pointed remarks about James's presence in her home.

Because of the build-up of paperwork over the weekend while she had been at home, she had no time for any lunch, and by the time she *was* actually able to leave, almost an hour later than usual, her stomach was grumbling protestingly.

She still had to pick Charlie up from Heather's, get home, make a meal, then get ready for their aerobics class, and as she knocked on Heather's back door she was already starting to apologise for her lateness when her friend opened it.

'Oh, but Charlie isn't here,' Heather told her, frowning. 'He told Danny his father was picking him up.'

Cursing James under her breath, Win headed back to her car. Slamming the door as she got in did little to relieve her pent-up emotions, and neither did accidentally stalling the engine as she tried to start it.

The amused glance of a male passer-by brought a flush of mortified colour to her face. Calm down, she warned herself as she re-started the car. Just calm down.

Easier said than done.

It didn't help to walk into the kitchen and find James and Charlie sitting comfortably either side of the table demolishing what looked suspiciously like the last portion of her home-made lasagne. Grimly eyeing the empty container, Win remembered that she had planned to eat it for her own supper.

'Enjoyed it, did you?' she demanded sourly as she shrugged off her jacket.

Charlie gave her a surprised look, and instantly she was ruefully aware of how unlike her normal self she was being.

'Sorry,' she apologised, ruffling his hair. 'I'm just feeling a bit fraught.'

She paused, suddenly conscious of the way James was looking at her. Against her will she turned to look back at him.

'Hard day?' he asked her.

That couldn't really be genuine concern and sympathy she could see in his eyes, she warned herself. He was simply digging yet another pit for her to hurl herself into.

'You could say that,' she agreed tersely. 'And it wasn't helped by the fact that I had to go out of my way to pick Charlie up from Heather's only to find he'd been picked up from school by his father.' She turned back to Charlie. 'You could have rung me to let me know, you know, love.'

She had always tried her best to instil an awareness of others and a sense of responsibility into her son, without overburdening him with it, and Charlie knew that if he ever needed to change any of the arrangements he made he should always ring her to let her know. It was, she had always told him, only good manners, and it showed consideration and awareness for other people. It was just as important, more important, she insisted, to show good manners to those closest to you as it was to outsiders. 'Do as you would be done by,' she had told him, but now her heart was touched with guilt and anxiety as he hung his head and kicked at the leg of his chair while he apologised to her.

'Sorry, Mum.'

It wasn't really his fault, it was James's, she told herself as she started to turn away, and then, as though he had read her thoughts, she heard James himself saying firmly,

'No, it was my fault, and I apologise for it, Win. I did think of phoning, but after what you said on Saturday evening I thought the last thing you'd want would be me ringing up the hotel and asking to speak with you. If your boyfriend...'

Rigid with anger, Win turned round.

'Tom does not operate the switchboard, and in the circumstances, even if he did, I'm sure he'd understand the reason you wanted to speak with me.'

As she said it she knew it was a lie. Tom would *not* have understood, or rather he would have chosen not to understand. However, that scarcely mattered now—now that she had been forced to acknowledge the impossibility of their relationship continuing.

'You're going out tonight, aren't you, Mum?' Charlie interrupted her thoughts. 'Only Dad and I have got this video...'

'Boyfriend again?' James asked softly. 'For a supposedly concerned mother, you do seem to have to rely on others rather a lot to take over your responsibilities for you. What had you got planned for Charlie tonight? Another overnight stay somewhere?'

Win was furious, but, all too aware of Charlie's bright-eyed interest in what was going on, she had to control herself until she had sent him upstairs on the pretext of cleaning his teeth before she could give vent to her feelings.

'For your information, I am *not* seeing Tom tonight, but going to an aerobics class with a friend and, as for Charlie, he normally comes with me.'

There was a small pause before James rallied, 'Likes aerobics, does he?'

Win audibly ground her teeth.

'Charlie goes swimming with Danny. The leisure centre has a swimming-pool—and, before you say a word, Charlie has his advanced certificate and his diving and life-saving certificates, and there's always a qualified lifeguard on duty at the pool. You see, *I* don't encourage him to sit at home watching television videos.' She gave him a bitter look. 'Something you would have known had you bothered to consult me before getting him one. I've been solely responsible for Charlie all his life, James,' she added bitterly. 'And if you think you can walk in here and tell me how to treat my own child . . .'

'Our child,' James corrected her.

His mouth had gone very thin, she noticed, and then she noticed something else, her heart thumping with heavy dread as she realised that beneath his self-control he was almost as angry as she was herself. The atmosphere in the kitchen was, she realised, as explosive as a still hot summer sky—sullen, ominous, heavy with tension, so that suddenly her skin felt clammy, her body heavy, her muscles tight, and then abruptly the fight left her, leaving her feeling limp and drained, too exhausted almost to move, never mind to argue.

Tiredly she pushed past James and opened the kitchen door, her chest still tight with tension, her body shaking inside.

With James's accusation still ringing in her head, Win cut short her evening, leaving the leisure centre immediately after her class had finished, not even waiting to shower and change, and shaking her head when Heather suggested they go for a coffee and a chat before going home.

'Sorry, I can't.' She pulled a wry face. 'I shouldn't be out at all,' she added bitterly. 'It's very irresponsible of me when I've got a child at home.'

Heather gaped at her.

'What? Irresponsible—you? Who on earth . . . ?'

'James,' Win told her fiercely, and then added quickly, 'Heather, if I start talking about it now, I'll probably never stop. I swear if he suggests just one more time that I'm neglecting Charlie in some way, I'll . . .' She shook her head, tears shining brightly in her eyes, and Heather, who had never seen her so visibly upset, stared at her in dismay.

'Hey, come on. You need to stay and have a drink, if only to help you calm down a little.'

'The class was supposed to do that,' Win told her wryly, 'and I can't stay. Why is it, Heather, that we women are so prone to guilt? I know I've done the best I possibly can for Charlie. All right, so I may not be perfect, but who is? And in just a handful of days, James has managed to turn me from a reasonably calm, self-assured, mature adult into an insecure, incompetent bundle of nerves who's beginning to seriously doubt that she's ever been fit to have charge of a child.'

'Rubbish!' Heather told her shortly. 'I don't know anyone who's a better mother than you. Even Rick's mother thinks you're wonderful,' she added feelingly.

Win managed to laugh, knowing how her friend felt about her rather domineering mother-in-law and her impossibly high and extremely impractical standards.

It was while she was in the car that Win started to shiver. She turned on the heater, blaming the fact that she must have got overheated while she was exercising and that it was rushing home without pausing to shower that was responsible for the tremors in her limbs.

They had nothing to do with the thought of facing James, of course. How could they? How indeed?

Her body felt stiff and sore when she climbed out of the car. She walked uncomfortably into the kitchen and then into the sitting-room. Charlie was seated on the settee next to his father, watching the television.

'Shush, Mum,' he commanded when she spoke to him, not taking his eyes from the screen. 'It's just getting to the good bit.'

So much for rushing back from the leisure centre to be with him, Win reflected as she walked back to the kitchen and looked longingly at the kitchen chairs. She was aching to sit down, but if she did she doubted if she would be able to find the energy to get up again, and she still had the ironing to do. Groaning under her breath, she walked over to the sink and switched on the coffee machine.

'You go and sit down—I'll do that for you.'

The unexpectedness of realising James had followed her into the kitchen shocked through her. She turned round to look at him, her face completely unguarded, wondering why he was looking at her so oddly, so compulsively almost.

Defensively she touched her face, suddenly realising how she must look, her hair damp with sweat, like the leotard she was wearing beneath her tracksuit.

'I came back without showering,' she said awkwardly. 'I thought Charlie...'

'Charlie's fine with his video. What do you mean, you came back without showering?' Suddenly he was frowning at her. 'Surely you know how important it is to take proper care to cool down and relax after exercising...the damage you can cause by neglecting to do so?'

Win swallowed. The room was beginning to swim sickly in front of her, her body was weak with exhaustion, her muscles trembling as though in confirmation of what James had just said. Of course she *knew* the importance of cooling down properly, but tonight getting back to Charlie had seemed more important.

She lifted a tired hand to her hair, pushing her fingers into its thickness. 'I...I didn't think.' The words were husky and too soft, and she had no idea why on earth she had voiced them.

'No, you always were impetuous.'

James's voice had changed as well. Win's senses registered the fact even though her brain was too exhausted to be able to analyse the reason for the change.

'Look, why don't you take this off? You're far too overheated.' Dizzily she felt James touch her hot face with the back of his hand as though testing the temperature of her skin.

She *was* hot—hot and uncomfortably sticky, hot and tired...hot and miserable, and hot and...

She protested sharply as she felt him tug down the zip of her tracksuit top, but he ignored her, deftly unfastening it and pushing it off her shoulders.

She wasn't sure which of them tensed first as he realised that all she had on underneath was a very fine cotton leotard, literally *all*—no top, no bra, nothing but a cotton so fine that it clearly defined the soft roundness of her breasts and even

the slight ridge that marked the outer circum-
ference of their areolae.

Win stiffened as she felt his fingers curl tensely
on her shoulders. Please God, don't let her body
remember that this man had once been her lover,
her husband, the father of her child...that he
had once turned her flesh as fluid as slow-flowing
honey; that he had once kissed and caressed every
single centimetre of her skin, that he had once
given her such pleasure that she had cried out in
wild abandonment to it. No, please don't let her
body remember that and betray her to him with
its memories of how he had once made her feel.

Her sharply indrawn breath broke the silence
between them. James released her, stepping back
from her, turning away from her. Quickly she
glanced down at her body, her face burning as
she saw the betraying hardness of her nipples.
She dragged her jacket around her, skirting past
James as she headed for the kitchen door, her
heart beating wildly with panic and despair.

The final seal on her day of disasters came just
before Charlie went to bed, when he informed
her that on Wednesday his school would be closed
for the whole day, due to some problem with the
heating system.

'I *did* tell you last week, Mum,' he reminded
her.

'I'm sorry, love, I must have forgotten. I'll ask
Heather if you can spend the day there with
Danny.'

'There's no need for that. Charlie and I can have a day out together, can't we, Charlie?'

Oh, God, why was fate playing so generously into James's hands? Fate was female, of course. She would have to be, wouldn't she? Win decided savagely as she bowed her head in defeat.

'We could go to Danelands,' Charlie was saying enthusiastically.

'Danelands?' James looked questioningly at Win.

'It's a new amusement park that opened last summer,' Win explained. 'The motorway goes right past it, and——'

'Mum promised to take me last year, but she didn't have time. Everyone else at school has been.'

Grimly Win forbore to remind Charlie that the reason they hadn't been was that they had spent a weekend at Centreparcs instead.

CHAPTER SEVEN

ON WEDNESDAY Tom announced that he had business meetings which would keep him away from the hotel for the rest of the day. He had said nothing about taking her out over the weekend, and Win suspected that he, like her, had decided that their relationship had to end.

Even though she knew she could not have married him, given his attitude towards Charlie, it still daunted her that he could let her go so easily. How much had he actually ever cared for her?

How much had she actually cared for him? No wonder the sex between them had been so lacking in fire. Since when had sex been important to her? she asked herself acidly while she worked. She had managed well enough without it for long enough, after all.

And surely having had her fingers, not to mention her heart, burned in its flames once had taught her what a very volatile and untrustworthy thing it actually was.

From her office she could look down into the hotel grounds. A couple strolled over the lawn below her, the man's arm round the woman's waist, her head resting on his shoulder. They paused, and she turned to smile at him as he said something to her.

They weren't a young couple, far from it, and suddenly Win's heart was heavy with longing and loneliness. Just for a moment she envied that woman more sharply than she had envied anyone in all her life. How wonderful it must be to have someone to care for you, someone you could trust, someone who would always be there for you. Someone to lean on? she mocked herself acidly.

Was that what she really thought a relationship should be about—the woman leaning on the man?

No, of course it wasn't, but just occasionally the thought of someone being there that she could actually *choose* to lean on if she wished...

Sighing, Win re-focused her attention on the screen in front of her, quickly tapping the necessary entry code into the computer so that she could cross-check on next week's bookings.

By pushing herself hard all morning, she managed to make enough time to take an hour off to go and do some shopping. Tonight she was going to make Charlie's favourite tea, and afterwards the two of them could go for a nice long walk together, just the two of them. After all, James would have had him all day. Impulsively she added a packet of Charlie's favourite chocolate biscuits to her trolley, ignoring the voice that nagged her about the importance of good nutrition, and the immorality of the kind of behaviour which advocated bribery as a means of buying loyalty.

While she waited in the queue at the check-out she tried not to dwell on the insidious and treacherous nature of her sex's apparent inborn inability to confront men with the reality of the subtle scoring-off game of destroying women's self-confidence which they seemed to enjoy playing so much. And Win had no doubt that James was enjoying putting her down as he skilfully manipulated both her and Charlie's emotions.

As always, she seemed to have managed to choose the wrong queue. Two women ahead of her sighed in exasperation as the cashiers changed over, further delaying them.

'Of course, you know what it is,' one was saying portentously to the other. 'If she hadn't left our Paul, none of this would have happened. Say what you like, a boy needs his father, especially when they get to that age. Mind, I'm not saying Stevie hasn't always been a bit of a handful, but this is the first time the police have been involved. Got off with just a warning, he has, but like I said to her...'

Irritated at herself for the *frisson* of despair-cum-guilt that shivered down her own spine as she listened to them, Win quickly pulled back from them, not wanting to hear anything more about the importance of fathers in their children's lives.

What about fathers who tainted and sometimes destroyed the lives of their children forever;
fathers who instilled in their daughters the
burdens of lack of self-esteem that came from a
deeply rooted childhood awareness of male contempt for their sex? What about the fathers who
taught their sons that women were not equals to
be treated with respect, but second-class citizens;
or, even worse, men who taught their sons and
their daughters that women fell into the two
ancient categories of whores or madonnas? What
about the fathers who abused their children and
who stole from them all their rights as human
beings?

With a small sense of shock, Win realised that
the check-out girl was waiting for her to unload
her trolley and that she was holding up the queue.
Red-faced, she filled the conveyor belt, her hands
clumsy and tense.

Of course, because she was in a hurry to get
home, the traffic would have to be particularly
bad; she had forgotten reading in the local news-
paper about the new roadworks starting at one
end of the town, and as she crawled slowly towards the bottleneck, she cursed herself for not
remembering in time and taking the long route
around the town. It might not have been much
shorter in time, but it would have been a good
deal less wearing on her nerves, and at least that
way she wouldn't have been sitting behind an

ancient truck billowing out clouds of choking
diesel fumes.

She desperately wanted to be home before
Charlie, miserably conscious that since she had
started work at the hotel her life had become so
busy and rushed that Charlie might well have
started to believe that he wasn't important to her
any more.

Not that he was the only boy in his class with
a full-time working mother, and he certainly
wasn't the only one from a one-parent family,
but she was guiltily aware of the contrast in their
lifestyle now that she worked at the hotel.

When her only means of earned income had
been the typing she did at home, she had always
been there for Charlie, waiting to welcome him
home from school, if she had not collected him
herself, with a glass of milk and his favourite
home-made biscuits, and with the time to sit
down and listen to him while he told her about
his day.

Now it was going on for six before she was
able to pick him up from Heather's, their evening
meal was often a rushed affair, with her listening
to Charlie with half an ear, while she frantically
tried to concentrate on all the tasks she had to
accomplish during the evening.

But she loved her job; loved the independence
it gave her, the feeling that she had a real place
in the world, the self-respect she had earned for
herself.

She sighed in relief as at last she was through the bottleneck.

How much would the ending of her private relationship with Tom affect her job? Would he expect her to leave? Certainly she doubted that he would continue with his original plans to give her more autonomy and responsibility. What would happen if James decided to challenge the court's ruling that Charlie should live with her?

Things had changed since the days when a judge would almost automatically grant custody to the mother. James was a wealthy man, certainly wealthy enough to provide a stable home life for Charlie. He could even marry again.

Her heart jerked painfully, causing her to tighten her grip on the steering-wheel. Why should the thought of James remarrying bother her so much? Was it really only because she felt so resentful of the imaginary young, energetic, pretty stepmother that James might potentially give her son? A stepmother who would be so much more fun, so much more available than a full-time working mother, a mother who no longer seemed in tune with the needs or the emotions of a teenage boy.

When she pulled up in front of the house and there was no sign of the Daimler, Win heaved a sigh of relief. With any luck she could have supper ready and her fraught nerves calmed enough for her to listen to Charlie's account of his day before they got back.

The house felt oddly empty and silent, and Win frowned as she registered this fact. It wasn't, after all, as though she wasn't used to Charlie not being here. He had a large circle of friends and a very active social life, something which she had always encouraged, provided she knew where he was and with whom, but as she got on with her preparations for supper she suddenly tensed, her body going stiff with rejection of the realisation that touched her.

It wasn't Charlie's voice she was listening for, not Charlie's thudding trainer-shod feet thundering up and down the stairs, but James's voice, James's firmer, more controlled presence.

She was missing him? After less than a week? Impossible! And why should she miss him anyway? He was the last person she wanted living with her.

Look at the havoc, the destruction his presence had already created. Her relationship with Tom was ruined, over. Her relationship with Charlie had been seriously undermined and damaged, and she was even beginning to think that Heather was starting to give her rather odd looks.

Don't get paranoid, she advised herself testily. She frowned as she put their meal in the oven and checked the time. They should be back by now, surely? Charlie had a good appetite, and it certainly wasn't like him to miss out on a meal.

Unless... Win stiffened suddenly, her face grim with anger. What if James had decided to prolong their day out by taking Charlie somewhere for a meal? But no, he must know she would be expecting them back. He had had Charlie for a whole day, which was more time than she had managed to spend with her son in heaven knew how many months, Win acknowledged unhappily.

Could she really blame Charlie if he preferred his father's company to hers?

She could see all too clearly how he might reason that at least his father wanted to be with him and made time for him, whereas his mother was always busy, always working...always out with Tom.

Win winced at her own thoughts. It was useless telling herself that an adult would quickly realise that James would soon tire of playing the indulgent father; that he would soon start to ignore Charlie as he had done when he was a baby, once he grew tired of playing this new role. Charlie was not an adult, and he could not be expected to see, to reason as one.

She glanced at the clock again. Was it really only ten minutes since she had last looked? Funny how time seemed to crawl so slowly when you were waiting for someone.

She went into the sitting-room intending to tidy up—then frowned as she opened the door.

The small room was immaculate, magazines, books, papers all tidied neatly away. The carpet had been vacuumed and the furniture polished.

The videos and games Charlie always seemed to leave scattered all over the place had been put neatly away; even the half-dead flowers had been removed from their vase and replaced.

Replaced. Win stared as she studied the clumsy arrangement in the jug, and suddenly for no reason at all she was remembering another evening just after she had announced her pregnancy. She had been out somewhere—to see her mother, perhaps. She had returned home feeling tired, aching all over, bewildered by the sheer magnitude of the conflicting emotions tormenting her, part of her aching to escape back into the simplicity of the way her life had been before she had met James, the other part...the other part aching with even more intensity for James to tell her that he still loved her and that he wanted their child.

Then too she had walked into this room expecting to find the untidy mess in which she had left it before she went out. Then too the room had been cleaned and tidied as if by magic; then too there had been fresh flowers in this jug which James had bought for her one weekend at a flea market when she had fallen in love with its faded colours.

Then too she had looked at the flowers with the most enormous lump in her throat and had been seized by emotions so strong that her body had shaken with the force of them, and yet, when James had come downstairs and walked into the sitting-room, instead of throwing herself into his arms as she had so longed to do, she had stared aggressively at him and demanded, 'Oh, I see ... trying to make me feel guilty, are you, just because I didn't stay in and do the housework? Well, I don't care what you think, James. I don't care at all, and I don't care about you any more either.'

She had stormed upstairs, to fling herself down on their bed, shaking with the shock of what she had said and done, praying that James would come up after her; but he hadn't. Instead he had gone out. She had heard the front door slamming after him.

She had been in bed but not asleep when he came back. He hadn't spoken to her, hadn't made any attempt to touch her.

With a faint sigh, Win came back to the present. Lightly she touched the petals of the flowers. They needed rearranging. She picked up the jug and carried it through into the kitchen.

There was no point in questioning why James had bought them. Certainly not to please her.

Once she was satisfied with their re-arrangement she carried them back into the sitting-room. Although small, it was a pretty room. She and Charlie had redecorated it the previous year, painting the walls a soft butter-yellow. They had experimented with sponging them, and Win was rather pleased with the effect they had created.

She had made new covers for the furniture and new curtains as well, and, although when she and James had first married she had rather disdained the second-hand pieces of furniture they had been given by both their families and would have preferred something far more modern, now she enjoyed polishing the rich patina of the wood, seeing it gleam with love and care, appreciating the solid practicality of furniture which had been in use when her own grandparents were young and which carried the scars to prove its suitability for family life.

She frowned as she glanced out of the window. Still no sign of James and Charlie.

By nine o'clock, when the meal she had prepared had long since been removed from the oven and thrown away, Win had gone through impatience and anger and had started to pace the floor, one eye anxiously on the telephone, her body clenched against the dread that attacked every person who had ever waited for someone to come home, knowing they were late beyond a reasonable amount of time, their mind filled with mental images of road accidents and tragedies.

If anything like that had happened, surely she would have known about it by now, she told herself. Surely someone . . . the police . . . ?

And yet if James had merely decided to extend their day out why hadn't he telephoned to let her know? She knew he did not have a car phone, but there were such things as public telephones;

some of them must have escaped the attention of the vandals, surely?

Mentally she willed the phone to ring, but it remained rebelliously silent. Perhaps she should ring the police? Perhaps...

She tensed as she heard a car coming down the road, then flew to the sitting-room window. The emotions that filled her as she saw James's Daimler come to a halt behind her own small car were too complex for true analysis, but the strongest of all of them was the anger that boiled up inside her as she watched the calm, relaxed way in which James got out of the car and walked with Charlie towards the house.

She had the door open before they reached it, but her furious 'Where have you been?' was. forestalled by James apologising lightly, as though they were a matter of minutes rather than a matter of hours late,

'Sorry about the delay, but there was a spot of bother on the motorway.'

A spot of bother? Her emotions burning scarlet patches of angry colour along her cheekbones, Win turned to castigate him, then saw that he was shaking his head at her and glancing meaningfully at Charlie's downbent head.

For the first time she realised how quiet Charlie was. When she looked properly at him, his face was pale—too pale.

Was he *ill*...sick? Was that why they had been delayed?

When, without speaking to her, Charlie pushed straight past her and stumbled upstairs, she stared after him in distress, but as she went to follow him James stopped her, his hand on her arm.

'Leave him,' he told her.

Leave him? Win's eyes mirrored all that she was feeling.

'He needs a few minutes to himself. There was a bad accident on the motorway and unfortunately Charlie witnessed some of it. A couple of cars ahead of us, travelling far too damn fast in not very good road conditions.'

'What happened?' Win asked him, still looking at the stairs. She ought to be with Charlie. She wanted to be with Charlie. She was his *mother*. He needed her...

As though she had spoken the words, she heard James saying quietly, 'He's not a child any more, or at least he doesn't think he is. Allow him the dignity of coming to terms with it by himself, Win. He's had a bad shock, but he's at that age when he believes that men don't cry.'

'What happened?' Win repeated. She felt sick and shaky herself now.

'One car skidded into the other, then burst into flames. There was nothing anyone could do. I pulled into the side and used the emergency phone to alert the authorities. 'We...I and a couple of other drivers who had stopped tried to help, but the flames... I wish to God Charlie hadn't been there with me.' As he turned his face away, Win

realised that it was streaked with smoke, that his
jacket sleeve was torn and his arm bandaged.

'It's nothing—just a minor burn,' he told her
dismissively. 'I would have rung you, but it just
wasn't possible. I had to stay to give a statement.'

He pushed his hand into his hair, suddenly
looking grey and tired. 'A whole family died in
one of the cars—mother, father and two small
children. A couple of young lads were in the
other. Dear God, why does it have to happen?'

'You said they were driving too fast,' Win reminded him automatically, the words meaning
nothing. She was too appalled by the mental pic-
tures he had drawn for her, by her awareness of
how close to danger both he and Charlie must
have been; by her awareness of the selfishness of
her own relief that her family was safe.

'Yes, they were, but knowing that isn't going
to help their families, is it? Do you know what
I was thinking afterwards as we drove back here?'
Win shook her head. 'I looked at Charlie and
imagined how I'd feel if I got that knock on the
door and someone telling me he'd been
killed... died like that, in the car that no doubt
I, as his father, had sanctioned him having. How
does anyone come to terms with that kind of
thing?'

Win couldn't speak. The raw pain in his voice
choked her.

'I need a bath,' he said with disgust. 'I stink
of smoke.'

But Win knew it wasn't the smell of smoke he wanted to wash away, but the smell of death.

'Charlie,' she said huskily. 'Should I . . . ?'

Immediately James shook his head.

'Leave him for tonight. Let him talk about it in his own time.'

It was only actually after he had gone upstairs that she realised that for the first time she had asked his advice, asked him to share with her her responsibilities as a parent, and not only that, but had genuinely needed his advice. And had acted on it?

She gave a tiny shiver, wrapping her arms around her body and desperately trying not to imagine herself in the place of those people who must tonight learn of the tragedy which had robbed them of those they loved.

It seemed a long time before James came back downstairs. When he did, he came into the kitchen, where she was simply standing staring into space, thinking about the years of Charlie's growing up, imagining how she would feel if she had heard tonight that his life was over.

'Charlie's gone to bed,' he told her. 'He's still in shock. I wish to God he hadn't had to be there with me. I know *I'm* going to have a hard time forgetting.'

'Children are very resilient,' Win heard herself saying, to her own surprise. 'And Charlie is still partially a child. They don't seem to have the propensity for transferring things like that to their own lives the way we do.'

'You mean Charlie isn't going to lie awake to-night thinking about how he'd feel if it was his son, his child, his wife in one of those cars? No, perhaps not, but I still wish he hadn't been there,' James told her grimly. 'If I hadn't allowed him to persuade me to stay for that last ride . . .'

'It wasn't your fault.'

What was she doing? Win asked herself numbly. Why on earth was she reassuring and comforting him? Why not do to him what he was constantly doing to her? Why not let *him* see how it felt to be made to feel guilty and inadequate as a parent? But she knew she could not turn such an appalling tragedy to her own advantage, not even in the war to win Charlie.

She realised that James was watching her and for some reason the expression in his eyes made her face go hot with self-conscious colour.

'Thanks,' he said softly, and for some reason the brief acknowledgement of her forbearance made her colour deepen.

The brief cool touch of James's fingers against her skin made her stiffen in shock.

'So you still do that. Amazing.' He didn't look amazed. He looked if anything faintly brooding. 'It's been a long day,' he told her. 'I think I'll have an early night.'

CHAPTER EIGHT

IT WAS the sound of Charlie screaming that woke her. Win reacted instinctively, out of bed, and across the landing, pushing open Charlie's bedroom door with her eyes still half closed and her brain still numb with sleep, the sound of him crying taking her to his side as instantly as it had done when he was small.

When she walked in, he was still asleep, but as she reached out and smoothed his hair off his forehead he woke up and focused on her. There were tears in his eyes, and it needed no words for her to hold out her arms to him and hug him tightly to her, rocking him.

She could hear him telling her about the accident, the words pouring out, muddled and confused, but the emotion plain enough. She hadn't held him like this since he was a child, she recognised. He considered himself too big for cuddles and kisses now, and she had forced herself to respect his need to distance himself from her. Now it shook her how different his body felt, all sharp angles and bones, with none of the baby softness she remembered. A sharp pang struck her at the knowledge of how quickly he was growing up and away from her. Now, tonight, he needed her, but already she could feel him fighting for self-control, and when he started to pull away from her she let him go.

It was instinct more than anything else which as he turned away from her, obviously embarrassed and angry now about his show of emotion, made her say quietly, absently almost, as though it were nothing,

'Your dad told me how proud he was of you, Charlie, for the way you behaved.'

'Yes, Charlie, I was.'

Win tensed, then turned round. When had James come into Charlie's bedroom? In the light from the landing she saw the smooth gleam of his chest, roughened with the soft dark hair she had once loved to touch. Beneath the hem of his robe, his legs were long and tanned. She remembered all too well how it had once felt to have the powerful muscles of his thighs flex beneath her hesitant exploration. How he had trapped her hand against his body and warned her, in that husky raw voice which had made her shiver in a mixture of pleasure and panic, just what she was doing to him and just what it made him want to do to her.

None of her previous boyfriends had ever talked to her so explicitly nor so erotically about sex, and somehow the sound of James's voice telling her how much he wanted to touch her skin, to kiss her breasts, to feel her tremble against him while he showed her all the ways in which he could give her pleasure, had aroused her so much that she had had to fight to stop herself from pleading with him there and then not just to tell her, but to show her.

James was speaking now. But not to her, to Charlie. Shocked with herself for what she was thinking, for allowing herself even for a second to be distracted from her son's pain, Win turned back to the bed.

'I *was* proud of you this evening, Charlie,' James was saying as he sat down beside their son. 'But not as proud as I am now.'

Charlie was looking at him, his need to conceal the tears he had been crying evident as he frowned at him.

'It takes a real man to admit that there are some things that happen in life which are so painful to us that they make us cry. That's where women have the advantage on us, Charlie. They aren't cowards like us, afraid of showing their emotions—and it *is* sometimes cowardly not to admit how we feel.'

'Men don't cry,' Charlie contradicted him flatly.

There was a brief silence, then James told him, 'This one does.'

Win held her breath as Charlie studied him. Like her, she could see that Charlie knew he was speaking the truth.

'Don't ever be afraid of your emotions, Charlie,' James told him. And then Win watched with tears blurring her own eyes as James reached down and wrapped his arms around his son, holding him. After a few seconds Charlie returned the embrace, tentatively at first and then with real emotion.

Quietly Win walked out of the bedroom, closing the door behind her and leaning against the landing wall.

This was what she had ached and longed for all those years ago when Charlie had been conceived, when he had been born; that James would love him and that he would show his love for him. But now that he had...

She heard the bedroom door opening and knew that James was standing behind her. It was only as she turned her head towards him that she realised that somehow the buttons of her top had become unfastened and the light was gleaming on the soft curve of her breast.

By some alchemy which brought her instant shocked despair, her body responded to that awareness, her nipples suddenly peaking into hard points that pressed against their thin covering.

In the half-light James's eyes gleamed slightly. He closed Charlie's bedroom door, his head inclining slightly towards her as he told her, 'No wonder your hotel owner wants you so much. Is it as good with him as it always was with us, Win?'

For a moment shock immobilised her vocal cords, and then as she fought free of it she demanded shakily, 'You have no right to ask me that kind of question—and, for your information, my relationship with Tom is based on far more than just sex ...'

Appalled, Win stopped. What on earth was she doing, saying? She had no relationship with Tom ... not any longer.

'So it isn't as good.'

The quiet words shivered through her, forcing her to push down her confusion as to why she had lied, forcing her to recognise her own danger and to deal with the very male satisfaction she had suddenly caught in James's voice.

'When I met you I was a *girl* ... a child.'

'You were no child in my arms, Win.' For some reason he sounded angry. 'And besides,' he added more softly, 'it's a well known fact that women don't even begin to reach their sexual peak until they're at least thirty.'

It was impossible to entirely eradicate the fine thrill of sensation that galvanised her body. To punish herself for it, she told him fiercely, 'I've learned from my mistakes, James. Sex isn't that important to me any more.'

'No?'

The speed with which he caught hold of her caught her totally off guard. One moment they were standing opposite one another, two adversaries on a familiar battleground, the next she was in his arms, her body pressed close to his, so close in fact that she could feel the heavy thud of his heartbeat as though it were controlling the flow of her own blood as well as his, its beat drowning out the lighter, faster race of her own heart, its power overwhelming her. As he had once overwhelmed her, or rather as her love, her need, her desire for him had overwhelmed her.

Well, that wasn't going to happen again, she told herself, panic-stricken, but already her brain seemed to have gone into slow motion, capable only of registering the fact that one of his hands was no longer imprisoning her body against his, but was instead smoothing its way up over her shoulder and along her throat, lifting the heavy weight of her hair off her shoulder so that his thumb could rub slowly and so very, very dangerously along its curve, releasing a flurry of sensations at once so familiar and so explicit that her senses went into total panic. Yes, her brain had registered all those things, but it seemed incapable of doing anything about them, of ordering her body, her muscles to take any kind of evasive action.

In fact, her head suddenly seemed very heavy, as though she wanted to tip it forward, to lean on something. Her skin felt acutely sensitive, her breasts heavy, swollen-tipped with a familiar subtle ache.

'Does *he* do this for you, Win?' she heard James asking her huskily as his mouth caressed her skin, following the line of her shoulder, nuzzling her yearning flesh, releasing all the memories, the needs, the feelings she had thought she had dammed up so successfully and so permanently. 'Or this?' His lips touched her ear, his tongue stroking just behind it, his hands sliding into her hair, tipping her head back as he looked down into her face.

Somewhere at the back of her mind she heard a small voice urging her to move away from him, but her senses wouldn't let her. Instead they urged her to move closer to him; to let his body take the weight of hers as she felt the tantalising drift of his mouth across her skin, until it rested feather-light against her own, the tip of his tongue tracing its shape.

Once long ago he had kissed her like this. Win felt herself shudder, felt the hot silk warmth of his skin beneath her flat palms without knowing how her hands had come to be inside his robe; felt the frightening, dangerous pulse of her own aching need and marvelled that it could still exist when it had been so quiescent for so many years and that she had all but forgotten it had ever existed.

Almost…but not quite. No woman could ever totally forget the man who had made her feel like this, Win acknowledged dizzily as she tried to say James's name, to tell him not to touch her, to remind him that they were no longer lovers but enemies.

But somehow in trying to open her mouth to speak she had sent him the wrong message and instead of releasing her his hold on her tightened, one hand pressed flat against her scalp, the other in the small of her back, his mouth opening over hers as he responded to the invitation he seemed to think she had given him.

She had forgotten what it was like to be kissed with such intimacy by a man who knew her body and its moods and needs; a man who had known exactly how to arouse her and who it seemed could still do so.

'Win . . . Win . . .'

She could feel the heavy slam of his heartbeat, its message as sensually exciting to her too vulnerable body as the rough huskiness of his voice.

He was kissing her again, opening her mouth, making her shudder with pleasure as she felt the fierce thrust of his tongue. His hand left the small of her back and slid up over her ribcage, tugging impatiently at her top until he had freed the silken swell of her breast. She felt him exhale in sharp pleasure as he touched her, her own body trembling wildly in response. His hand actually seemed to tremble slightly as his thumb stroked over her nipple.

She tried to close her eyes to look away, but some sharp angle of the light made her glance down to where his hand lay against her skin. Her flesh was pale, soft, her breast swollen, creamy, the darkness of its areola a sharply erotic contrast to her skin's paleness.

She realised that James had removed his hand, that he was staring down at her body. In the dim light she caught the fierce gleam of his eyes and felt the sudden bound of his heart as he said her name, then bent to gather her in his arms, lifting her off her feet—carrying her, she realised in sudden panic, into the room in which he was sleeping. The room she had so long ago shared with him. The room she had no longer been able to endure sleeping in herself once she was alone.

She tried to protest, to bring some sanity back to the situation, but as he lowered her on to the bed his mouth was already caressing the soft slope of her breast, not hesitantly or exploratively but with all the determined seeking instinct of a man intent on one goal.

Her heart seemed to turn over inside her chest as she recognised the need that drove him. She could perhaps have stopped him, could have moved away, could have evaded that seeking, hungry male mouth, but by the time that thought had registered it was too late, and his tongue was licking fiercely at her tender flesh, his mouth fastening over her taut nipple, his face hot against her skin, his hands urgently impatient of the barrier of her nightshirt as he lifted her up against him, caressing the full length of her naked back.

Feelings, sensations, emotions she had thought it impossible for her ever to feel again swamped her. Without even knowing what she was doing, she started to make the small keening noises that the intimacy of being caressed by him like this had always caused her to make.

Until James had come into her life, she had had no idea that it was possible for a woman to feel that kind of desire, that kind of need, and at first she had been shocked and embarrassed by it, but then James had taught her, shown her how much pleasure it gave him to see her sensual response, and gradually she had learned to let go of her self-consciousness and her self-control, and now it seemed that her body remembered those lessons far too well.

Dizzily she tried to resist the tide of sensations drowning her, to remind herself of all the reasons why this should not be happening, but in the light through the uncurtained window she could see the satin-velvet gleam of James's skin, and the darkness somehow accentuated the aroused male scent of his body, at once so familiar and so erotic that she ached to bury her face against him and to breathe it in, to run her hands over him, to touch and stroke him; to taste each familiar texture of his flesh. She was like someone who had been on a strict diet suddenly confronted with the opportunity to gorge herself on all the forbidden delights, she acknowledged hazily, and like any sane and sensible dieter she ought to resist; for one thing, she was simply not used to such richness and it could all too easily make her very, very sick indeed... But James had transferred his attention to her other breast, and the sharp fire darts of pleasure that seemed to tug on her womb in much the same way that his mouth did on her breast obliterated her ability to think.

She slid her hands beneath his robe, glorying in the sensation of feeling his skin beneath her palms, of knowing that its heat, its dampness was caused by his desire for her. She felt his hand cup her hip and then caress her thigh, and immediately the ache inside her body intensified. She shivered as he touched her, knowing that already he would find her body moist and welcoming.

How long had it been since she had felt like that? Certainly never with Tom. Not even...

James was kissing her midriff, her waist, the rounded curve of her belly, while his hands held her thighs. She knew what he was going to do and shuddered tensely in confused despair. This should *not* be happening. She should not be here like this with him. It was wrong, dangerous. She would be hurt again the way she had been before.

The words ran through her brain like a refrain, but her body had slipped her mind's control. With frightening clarity she perceived a truth which she had successfully concealed from herself for years.

She still loved him.

The knowledge was like a blow against her heart, immobilising her will-power and her ability to fight. Her whole body had become a weak, trembling ache of need. She could hear James talking to her, the words husky, rough with passion.

It had shocked her at first, this way he had of talking to her while they made love, of telling her how desirable he found her, of how beautiful he found each and every part of her body. Her breasts, he had told her, made him ache with pleasure, her nipples were like tiny perfect pale pink roses that flowered in the moist heat of his mouth. That had been before she had had Charlie. She wondered what he thought of them now—now that they were a woman's and not a girl's.

When she had trembled violently as he kissed the inside of her thighs he had laughed gently at her and told her that that was nothing to the pleasure she would have when he kissed her more intimately, but despite his laughter she had seen the passion, the arousal in his eyes, and her body had leapt in response to the knowledge that she had the power to arouse him so intensely.

Then, as he had slowly and patiently coaxed her to allow him the intimacy of slowly and delicately caressing the most private part of her body, she had been uncertain, half afraid, of both him and herself as well as the pleasure he had promised her, resisting the shocking force of it, fighting her own need to abandon herself to it.

Now too she fought to resist it, but for different reasons—but no amount of trying to clench her muscles and think of something . . . anything else could stop the sharply piercing sweetness engulfing her.

As she fought to stay still and not to give in to the need to twist and writhe, to cry out her pleasure and her need, she heard James saying thickly to her, 'Oh, God, you even still taste the same—sweet, like honey.'

Then she felt his mouth on her and her control broke.

Later, wrapped in his arms, her body just that little bit tender from his possession of it, from the sheer unfamiliarity of any kind of sexual intimacy, she was still trembling with disbelief at what had happened.

'Now,' James told her as his mouth caressed the damp hollow at the base of her throat, 'tell me again that you're going to marry someone else, and give my son a new father. He doesn't want this hotel owner in his life, Win—you know that, don't you?'

Suddenly she was icy cold, her body rigid with the freezing sharpness of awareness and knowledge.

James hadn't made love to her because he wanted her. He hadn't as she had so stupidly, so idiotically thought, suddenly been overwhelmed by desire for her, by need for her. It hadn't been the shock of witnessing such a horrific accident

or the distress it had caused Charlie that had
driven him to make love to her. He had done it
simply and cold-bloodedly to undermine her, to
use her own vulnerabilities against her.

She tried to imagine how she might be feeling
right now had she still been planning to marry
Tom. Her stomach churned with nausea and self-
contempt. She pushed herself away from him,
trying not to wince at the betraying tenderness
inside her body, trying not to remember how after
he had stroked and kissed her, after he had
aroused her to a state of almost unbearable
longing and urgency, he had slowly made love to
her, filling her body with his, her acutely sensitive flesh pulsing with tiny sharp bursts of
pleasure at the sensation of his power and
strength moving against her tautly eager muscles,
sending them into a flurry of brief convulsions
which had made her cry out aloud and which had
made James, or so she had thought, abandon his
own self-control.

He had made love to her again after that,
seeming to know without her having to tell him
that she still ached for him; and this time it had
been she who whispered to him how much she
wanted to touch him, to stroke him, to kiss and
taste him and then to hold him deep within her
body.

Now she could hardly credit what she had
done, her face burning as she remembered all that
she had said, how she had whispered and pleaded,

how she had cried out to him her need, how she
had nearly done everything but tell him she still
loved him.

There wasn't much left that she could salvage,
but her pride demanded that she at least make
an attempt. She wasn't a girl any more, after all,
to shut herself away and cry because she had discovered that he didn't really love her.

'I know what you're trying to do, James,' she
told him shakily as she fumbled on the floor for
her nightshirt and hastily pulled it on. 'But you're
wasting your time.'

He had started to come off the bed after her,
but now abruptly he stopped. In the half-light
his face looked oddly pale, stripped of its warm
colour, bleached almost as though he was in
shock, or in pain.

It was just an illusion, Win told herself as she
turned her back on him and headed for the door.
Once there she paused and turned round.

'I know exactly why you've come back here,
exactly what you hoped to achieve, but it won't
work.'

'And tonight?' he asked her, his voice oddly
heavy, the words echoing hollowly with a
bleakness that made her shudder.

'Tonight never happened,' she told him
fiercely, curling her fingers into her palms as she
waited for him to deride her, to taunt her with
her vulnerability, with her love, but to her relief
he simply remained silent, watching her.

CHAPTER NINE

'AND tonight?'

'Tonight never happened.'

The words rang heavily through Win's head as she got up; a death-knell, but a death-knell to what? A love that had never existed, at least not on James's part. She felt heavy-eyed, her brain dulled, her body lethargic, aching for the sleep it had been denied.

She woke Charlie and, seeing his white face and huge eyes, debated whether she ought to keep him off school as she went downstairs to start the breakfast.

She knew the moment James came into the kitchen, but she didn't turn round, ignoring both him and the tiny prickle of sensation that made the hair lift at her nape. It wasn't quite as easy to ignore the dull ache in her body, nor the sharp pain in her heart.

How could she have loved him all these years and not known? She had spent what was left of the night trying to answer that question, trying to convince herself that because of her upbringing she had somehow managed to persuade herself that because she found him sexually desirable she must love him; but she had known it wasn't the truth. She wasn't a child any more, and she knew that had she felt the need to do so she would quite happily have had a discreet sexual relationship with a man she desired, without feeling any guilt at not actually loving him, had such a situation arisen. The mere fact that it had not told its own story.

Dear God, if only James had not chosen to come back into their lives, disrupting them, disturbing them.

Over breakfast, Charlie was unusually subdued. When he did speak it was to Win and not to James, although she didn't immediately recognise the significance of this fact. But when he asked her if she would take him to school, she gave him a concerned frown, too worried to even think of feeling victorious because it was her he wanted and not James.

'Can we go now?' he asked her, pushing away his cereal bowl with his breakfast barely touched. 'I—I want to walk.'

To walk? Win just managed to bite back the words and to stop herself from reminding him how he loathed walking to school.

She could feel James watching them both, and was helplessly aware that she was confronting a situation she had no experience of handling. Ought she to gently insist on driving Charlie there, or would that simply make matters worse? She could understand how traumatic witnessing such an appalling accident must have been, but how ought she to deal with his reaction to it? Should she simply act as though there were nothing unusual in his wanting to walk to school and for her to walk there with him, or should she try to talk to him about his reluctance to travel there in the car?

'Yes. Yes, of course we can walk,' she assured him as calmly as she could. She could feel James watching them both.

She glanced instinctively towards him, then wished she had not, as her skin burned with the burden of her memories of last night. He was frowning, no doubt disapproving of the way she was handling the situation.

'Charlie, your mother hasn't even finished her coffee yet,' she heard James saying quietly. 'Why don't you and I——'

'No. I want Mum to take me.'

Consternation filled Win as she saw the way Charlie's mouth trembled.

'That's all right,' she said quickly. 'I—I don't want any more coffee. Go upstairs and clean your teeth, Charlie, while I get my coat.'

For the first time since James had arrived, Charlie actually seemed relieved to get away from him, and Win was not really surprised when the moment the door had closed behind him James said grimly to her, 'You're not doing him any favours by pandering to him like this, you know. It won't make it any easier for him to get over what's happened.'

'What am I supposed to do? Force him to get in the car?' Win was trembling herself now, angry because she knew he was right and yet at the same time protective of her son.

'You're encouraging him to cling to you, to be over-dependent on you. You're encouraging him to believe that women are there to satisfy other people's needs. You could at least have made him wait until you'd had your coffee. You aren't doing him any favours, you know, Win—and you certainly aren't doing any for the woman who will ultimately share his life. Or are you never going to allow that to happen?'

The accusation was so unfair that it robbed her of breath.

'You're just jealous,' she told him emotionally. 'That's all it is. You're just jealous.'

And shockingly she saw from the dark surge of colour that crawled up under his skin that she was right. He even admitted it, his mouth hard and bitter as he told her acidly, 'Too damned right I am. But not half so much as that hotel-keeper of yours might be. No wonder he doesn't want Charlie around.'

He stormed out of the kitchen as Charlie came back into it, Charlie's pallor and obvious tension taking precedence over her initial confusion at James's gibe.

Walking Charlie to school caused her to run late, so that she didn't have time to do anything more than rush back into the kitchen to snatch up her keys and bag before running back out to her car and setting off for work.

It was the start of a very difficult week, with Charlie becoming progressively more and more demanding and James more and more withdrawn.

As Win admitted to Heather when they went to their aerobics class together, she had been in two minds as to whether she ought to cancel and stay at home.

'Charlie almost threw a tantrum when he knew I was coming out.' She frowned and looked at her friend. 'I just don't know what to do for the best, Heather.'

'What does James think?' Heather asked her.

'James?' queried Win.

'Well, he *is* Charlie's father, and you said yourself that Charlie was positively doting on him until this happened.'

'Yes. He—he thinks I should distance myself a little from Charlie, not let him be so clinging.'

'Not let him have quite so much control over your life, you mean,' Heather said shrewdly, smiling wryly at her when Win turned a shocked face to look at her.

'Oh, come on, Win, we've known each other long enough for us to be honest with each other, surely? Charlie is possessive about you, and it's perfectly understandable, but he's a strong-willed boy and he's not used to having anyone else but you in his life. I suspect he doesn't like the idea of having to share you with anyone, and that this accident, however genuinely terrifying it must have been for him, has simply given him, even if only subconsciously, a means of ensuring that he keeps you to himself.'

'But he doesn't have to share me with anyone,' Win protested. 'I know at one time I had thought that Tom and I—but...'

'Who's said anything about Tom?' Heather asked her softly.

Win stared at her, frowning at first, then her colour coming and going as Heather confirmed, 'Yes, I *did* mean James. I suspect now that the gloss, the excitement of having his father around is starting to wear off, Charlie is wising up a bit and beginning to realise that James isn't going to be as soft with him as you've always been, and that James isn't going to be as easy to remove from your life as the likes of Tom.'

'To remove from my life?' Win gasped. 'But he isn't *in* my life.'

'He's living with you, isn't he?' Heather pointed out remorselessly, adding gently, 'And you do still love him, don't you?'

Win winced. 'Is it so obvious?'

'Not really. Call it an inspired guess. Mind you, having seen him, I can't say I blame you,' Heather grinned mischievously. 'He *is* rather gorgeous.'

Win laughed, but her heart was heavy—not because her friend had guessed how she still felt about James, but because of what she had said about Charlie. She knew Heather too well and valued her opinion far too much to even begin to think that her friend was in any way being unfair or unkind. And if what she had said was true, then somehow, for Charlie's own sake, she was going to have to find a way to gently help him to accept that there was room in both their lives for them to love other people. But how?

She tensed a little as the first thing that came into her mind was that James would know how to deal with the situation, that James, another male, the closest male relation Charlie had, was bound to be able to help him through this turbulent patch of emotional trauma much better than she could herself.

But *if* she applied to James for help, wasn't he just going to turn round and say 'I told you so'? Wasn't he just going to use her own admission of weakness against her to reinforce his plan to take Charlie from her?

She knew that she could, if she wished now, use Charlie's vulnerability to bind him so close to her that he would shut James completely out of his life, but she also knew that to do so would be to severely damage Charlie himself, to prevent him from taking an important step towards maturity and adulthood. Charlie needed James. He needed his father.

There, she had finally admitted it.

But Charlie needed her as well. Which meant that it was up to James and herself to find some way of ensuring that Charlie remained in close contact with them both, and, even more important, to make sure that he did not suffer because of their hostility towards one another. Or rather James's hostility towards *her*, she reflected miserably. What she felt for him wasn't hostility at all, as Heather had pointed out.

Not that she had needed Heather to tell her how she felt about James. She had known that the moment he kissed her, the moment he touched her; and somewhere deep in her heart she had known it even before that. Had known it when he hurt her so badly by rejecting her and Charlie; had known it even when he had been unfaithful to her; had in fact *never* stopped loving him, no matter how hard she had tried.

And because she had not been able to destroy her love for him she had buried it, sealed herself off from it, tried to convince herself that it had never even existed.

She gave a small tense shudder. If only it had not. But if she had never loved James then she would never have had Charlie.

She rubbed her hand tiredly against her aching temple. Why did life have to be like this? So—so complex and so full of pain.

CHAPTER TEN

HAVING admitted to herself that she needed James's help and advice with Charlie was one thing, Win discovered; finding not just the courage but the opportunity to broach the subject with him was quite definitely another.

For one thing, James himself seemed more distant, more aloof, distancing himself from her so obviously that she knew he wanted to ensure she did not read the wrong meaning into the physical intimacy they had shared. Her body burned hot with chagrin and self-contempt whenever she remembered her own vulnerability and the reckless speed with which she had abandoned herself to her need, *her* love, and she knew that if she only had her own feelings, her own future, to consider, her pride would not have allowed her to make any approach to him at all. But there was Charlie. And Charlie's needs, Charlie's future were far more important to her than her own pride. Charlie was after all the reason that James had come here in the first place.

And James *must* care about him, must love him, for him to put up with the way Charlie had been behaving ever since the accident. Win winced as she thought about her son's rudeness, and her own apparent inability to get through to Charlie that what he was doing was wrong and unfair.

The truculence he had begun to display towards her was all now directed towards James. Where once he had hung almost slavishly on James's every word, he now virtually ignored him. He had even begun to be almost aggressively reluctant to leave James alone with her, and Win was finding it harder and harder to ignore Heather's warnings.

And James—James who had been so impatient and unsympathetic of a small baby's crying—had amazed her with his tolerance of Charlie's rudeness and aggression now. In fact, if anything he seemed to be far more tolerant of Charlie's behaviour than she felt herself, and far more patient with him as well.

She had tried to talk with Charlie both about the accident and about his behaviour, but his response to her attempts was so negative that she had had to abandon the discussion.

Heather commiserated with her when she telephoned her to discuss the problem with her.

'If you like, I could ask Rick to have a chat with him,' Heather offered, but Win vetoed her suggestion. She couldn't help thinking how hurtful it would be to James to know that his son preferred to talk over his problems with another man. But why should she care how much James was hurt? He had never cared how much he hurt her, had he?

As though fate was determined to make things as difficult as possible for her, she was having problems at work as well. Tom had become hyper-critical of her work—unfairly so, she felt— and when he was in the office with her he often made unsubtle gibes about the fact that she and James were living under the same roof.

She tried to be as fair as possible and not to let her own feelings blind her to the fact that Tom's reactions were perhaps to be expected in the circumstances, but he had recently started dating one of the new part-time receptionists, a girl whom Win had taken on half against her own judgement because they had been desperate for extra staff, and now she was discovering that this girl's relationship with Tom was making it very difficult for her to discipline her over her very lax attitude towards timekeeping and the number of errors in her work.

Win had tried to point out to her that by arriving late and leaving early she was in fact making things very difficult for her co-workers, but to no avail, and now this afternoon she had simply not turned up for work at all, and they were so busy that Win had had to work on the reception desk herself.

Thoroughly disheartened, she was beginning to wonder whether she had any real right to be in this kind of a job when she couldn't even get her own son to understand the importance of tolerance and good manners and of trying to see the other person's point of view, never mind the staff working under her.

It was late by the time she managed to leave the hotel, almost seven o'clock. She felt tired and drained, harassed to the point where her own temper was in danger of snapping, knowing that in the morning she would have to confront Lisa with the alternative of either conforming to the rules or thinking about looking for another job, and knowing equally that when she did so Lisa was all too likely to throw down her relationship with Tom as a gauntlet between them. She was that kind of girl.

Tiredly Win got out of her car, walked up the front path, and opened the front door.

Charlie and James were both in the kitchen. Charlie was sitting at the table glaring mutinously at James, a plate of congealed food on the table in front of him. The hostility emanating from him was almost visible, and Win's heart sank as she saw the anger and stubbornness in his eyes and the grim determination on James's face.

'What's wrong?' she asked quietly, trying to take a deep calming breath.

'He says I've got to eat this, and I don't want to,' Charlie told her.

Win's heart sank even further. A glance at the plate had shown her that it contained one of Charlie's favourite meals.

'It's bad manners to refer to anyone as "he" or "she", Charlie,' she began automatically. 'Why don't you want your gammon? It's one of your favourites.'

'It's cold,' Charlie told her unnecessarily.

Across the table from him, James drew in his breath. Win heard it and mentally acknowledged his right to feel irritation, but Charlie was looking at her pleadingly, and behind the defiance in his eyes she could see the same appeal for her support that she had seen when he was still small and helpless and totally dependent on her.

She steeled herself to harden her heart against it. Charlie knew very well how to get round her, and he wasn't helpless or dependent now.

'Well, whose fault is that?' she asked him.

She almost flinched at the way he looked at her; as though she had betrayed him in some way; as though she were a traitor.

'He didn't cook it the way I like it. I wanted you to cook it. You *said* you'd be home early.'

'I said I'd try to be home early, Charlie,' Win corrected him. 'I'm sorry I couldn't be, and your gammon looks perfectly all right to me.'

She wanted to remind him of how much he had wanted James in his life, of how he had deliberately deceived her because of that need, but she couldn't do so with James there with them.

Instead she said quietly, 'It was very good of your father to make your supper for you, and——'

'I didn't *ask* him to make it,' Charlie interrupted her before she could finish her sentence. 'I don't want him here—interfering, telling me what to do. It was better when it was just you and me, Mum.'

Before Win could say anything he had pushed back his chair and was leaving the kitchen. She knew she ought to call him back and make him apologise to James, but she simply didn't have the strength.

When he had gone, she turned to James and said unevenly, 'James, I'm sorry. I——'

'Are you?' he interrupted her savagely. 'I don't think so. After all, you've always made it clear that you don't want me to be a part of his life.' He got up abruptly. 'I have to go out.'

When he had gone, Win picked up the plate of congealed food and disposed of it. She heard Charlie coming back downstairs and into the kitchen, but she deliberately kept her back to him as she washed the greasy plate.

'What's wrong, Charlie?' she asked when she had finished. 'I thought you wanted your father here.'

Charlie scowled at her.

'I did at first, but I don't now. I want it to be just the two of us, like it was before. I don't want anyone else living here with us. Mum, if anything happened to you, if... if there was an accident, I wouldn't have to go and live with him, would I?'

Where once Win would have rejoiced to hear those words, now they made her heart ache, for Charlie and for James as well. She went over to him, kneeling down beside his chair and putting her arms around him, hugging him, resting her chin on top of his head as she told him softly, 'Charlie, I can't promise never to be in an accident, although I do promise I shall try my best not to be. You're old enough to understand now that, if anything should happen to me, your father is legally your next of kin, but I know he wouldn't want you to be unhappy any more than I would. You know, don't you, that you could always choose to live with Gran and Grandad, or with one of your uncles?'

'But they all live far away. I want to stay here,' Charlie told her.

'Your Aunt Heather has always promised me that she would take care of you if you wanted that. *Is* that what you'd want, Charlie, to go and live with Danny?'

'I don't want to live with anyone but you,' he told her passionately, and Win hugged him tightly.

'I know, love, I know,' she comforted him. She also knew where these fears had come from and how deeply the accident had affected him.

'I don't want you to get married again, Mum, and have other children. I just want it to be you and me forever.'

'Oh, Charlie!'

What could she say? Promise never to remarry? It was highly unlikely that she would—not now she had realised how she felt about James; but to make that kind of promise to Charlie would be wrong.

It must have been late when James returned, because she didn't hear him. His car was outside when she got up in the morning, but there was no sign of him before she left for work.

She managed to make time for a very brief lunch-hour and drove round to see Heather to discuss what had happened with her.

'Mm. Sounds to me as if he's suffering a very bad dose of pubescent male jealousy. They all go through it, apparently, rebelling against the authoritative male figure. It's just that in Charlie's case it's so much worse because he considers that he is the male head of the household.'

'He was so rude to James, and so...so hurtful,' sighed Win.

'Have you discussed it with James yet?' Heather asked her.

Win shook her head.

'He...he went out last night and I was in bed when he came back. I feel so guilty, Heather. He

seems to think I'm deliberately trying to turn
Charlie against him, and I'm not. In fact...'

'In fact you'd welcome some support from him
in dealing with Charlie,' Heather suggested.

'Yes. I feel I'm failing Charlie in some way.
That if he felt secure and self-confident he
wouldn't have this need to shut other people out
of his life. I *know* it's partially due to witnessing
that accident, but...'

'But it worries you that Charlie doesn't want
to share you with anyone else, not even his own
father.'

'Yes,' Win agreed. She glanced at her watch.
'Oh, God, look at the time. I must get back.'

For once she managed to leave work on time.
There was no sign of the Daimler when she pulled
up outside the house, but she knew James was
looking at various commercial properties with a
view to finding a suitable home for his business.

Charlie was just on the point of going out. He
was going round to see Danny, he told her.
Reminding him not to be too late, Win took off
her coat and started to make herself a cup of
coffee.

It was only when she sat down that she saw
the note on the table. It was in James's hand-
writing. As she picked it up, her stomach started
to churn sickly. She slit the envelope and read
the letter inside quickly, knowing that half of her
had guessed even before she read it just what it
would say.

He had decided it would be best for him to move out of the house, he had written. He had booked himself into a local hotel. It was obvious to him that his presence was upsetting Charlie, and for the boy's sake he had decided that perhaps he ought to think again about returning to live locally.

The denial that broke in Win's throat was stifled by the hand she had placed in front of her mouth. Tears burned her eyes as panic, misery and anger—an anger more intense than anything she had ever known before in her whole life, more intense even than the rage she had experienced when she had discovered James's unfaithfulness—filled her.

She picked up the phone, quickly dialled Heather's number, and asked her friend if it was possible for Charlie to stay overnight with Danny.

'Something's come up,' she told her. 'Something important. Is Charlie there?'

Charlie was rebellious at first when she told him he was to spend the night with Danny, but this time she found the strength to be firm.

'Are you going out with Tom?' he asked her.

'No,' she told him. 'There's something I want to discuss with your father.'

She had to make several phone calls before she discovered where James was staying. Praying that he was actually in the hotel, she hurried out to her car.

It was only instinct that was impelling her to act with such urgency; instinct and the knowledge that both of them, both Charlie and James, would suffer if she allowed their relationship to be severed in this way.

Luckily the hotel receptionist was inexperienced, and when Win announced herself as Mrs Gardner she was quite happy to give her James's room number and a key.

Her heart thumping, Win headed for the lift. This wasn't something she could ever have done for herself; she could imagine how James would receive her, how little he would want to see her and to hear what she had to say, but she wasn't fighting for her own happiness now—she was fighting for Charlie's, and for Charlie's future, and, no matter what Charlie might think or say now, he needed his father in his life. He needed the love James had for him.

And James did love him—he must do, to have put what he thought Charlie wanted before his own desire to be a part of Charlie's life.

He did not love *her*, but he did love Charlie. That was what she was banking on, *praying* for. Where once she would have fiercely denied that James felt anything for his son, and been glad to make that claim, now she was hoping that, somehow over the years, James's emotions had undergone a change and that he now did love the son he had rejected.

She knocked on the door, then unlocked it.

James was just coming out of the bathroom, tucking his shirt into his trousers, his hair damp, and for a moment, at the sight of him, Win's love for him made her go weak with need, no other thought in her head but how much she longed to go up to him and touch him, hold him, beg him to stay with her—then she reminded herself why she was here and forced herself to meet his eyes.

It was obvious that he was surprised to see her. Surprised and—displeased?

'Win! What——?' he began.

'I've come to talk to you about Charlie,' she told him quickly before he could say anything; before he could deny her and ask her to leave.

She saw the way his mouth twisted.

'I think we've said it all—or rather Charlie's said it for us—don't you?'

'He needs you, James. Oh, I know it may not seem that way. I know he himself may not even realise it. He's going through a very difficult patch at the moment, and...well, he isn't exactly used to having another male presence in his home, but——'

'No buts, Win. He's not a child, not really, and he's made his views very clear. I suppose I can't entirely blame him. In his shoes no doubt I'd feel exactly the same way. I suppose I should have seen the warning signs when he wrote to me and told me he didn't want you marrying your hotel owner. I thought then it was because he was afraid the guy might mistreat him in some way, that he might lose out to the children you might have with him. Stupid of me, I suppose, to think that——' He broke off, his mouth suddenly hardening. 'But then I suppose none of us are ever too old to behave stupidly, are we?'

Win flushed, wondering if he was referring to the night they had made love, but she wasn't going to allow herself to be embarrassed into backing down, not with Charlie's happiness at stake.

'Can't you see, James, the very fact that he's behaving in the way he is proves how much he needs you in his life? You rejected him when he was a baby. Please don't reject him now.' She took a deep breath. 'When you turned up here, I'd have done anything to turn Charlie against you. The last thing I wanted was you in his life, but now——'

'But now you've begun to see that it might have certain advantages.' James interrupted her sardonically. 'Like why not let me take the flak, so that you and Tom can build a nice cosy life for yourselves without Charlie breathing down your necks.'

'No!' Her denial was immediate and vehement. Her eyes flashed anger and disbelief as she fought to control her emotions. 'I love Charlie,' she told him fiercely. 'How dare you even suggest——?'

'*You* might love him, but your fiancé most certainly doesn't, does he?' James challenged her.

'My...my what?' Win stared at him, confused. 'Tom and I aren't engaged. In fact——'

'In fact what?' James pressed.

Shrugging mentally to herself, Win decided that she might as well tell him the truth. It made no difference now anyway.

'Tom and I realised some time ago that it just wasn't going to work. I knew Charlie wasn't very keen on him, but I had no idea just how antagonistic towards him he was until...'

'Until I turned up on your doorstep. He must have really hated him, eh, to have turned to me, his despised and unwanted father, for help——'

Win flushed at the derision in his voice.

'Charlie has never despised you,' she told him in a low voice. 'In fact, if anything, he's rather hero-worshipped you. I think that's partially why he's behaving so...so badly now.'

'Discovered his idol's human after all, is that it?'

'The accident upset him, James. He asked me last night what would happen to him if I...if I had an accident.'

'And what did you tell him?' James demanded grimly. 'That he need not come and live with me if he didn't want to?'

Her expression gave her away, and she flushed beneath the contempt in his eyes.

'Don't you *see*,' she appealed, 'that's why it's so important that you *are* a part of his life, that you form a proper bond with him, and . . .'

'A *proper* bond with him. That's going to be so easy, is it? Not once I'm back in Australia and he's here.'

Back in Australia. Win had to cling to the back of a chair for support. She could feel the blood draining down her body under the force of her shock. She wanted to cry, to plead, to cling to James and beg him to tell her she had misheard him, but fortunately her shock kept her immobile.

'It seems the best thing to do.' He had his back to her. 'Face it, Win. It might suit you now to have me in Charlie's life, but it certainly won't suit him—not while he thinks I'm some kind of threat to his relationship with you.'

Win stared at him. 'What do you mean?'

'I mean that Charlie, like any other male, is very adept at sensing any kind of threat to what he considers to be his territory. The reason Charlie doesn't want me in his life, Win, is that he doesn't want me in yours.'

Win could feel herself blushing. Was he trying to tell her he had guessed how she felt about him, and that it was as much because of that as anything else that he had decided to return to Australia?

Desperation lent her a strength she had never known she possessed.

'If you loved him, really loved him, you'd know how important it is that he learns to come to terms with those kind of negative emotions,' she told him fiercely. 'He needs you, James. He needs you to show him how to be a man... I *can't* show him that. He needs you even more now than he did when he was a baby. You turned your back on him then, please don't turn your back on him now. He's your son. I know you don't want me in your life, but Charlie——'

'*What*?'

The ferocity in the sharp word silenced her, confusing her, making her hesitate and look uncertainly at him.

'What did you just say?' he demanded.

'I...' Win licked her lips, suddenly conscious of how dry they were, of how tense she was, her muscles stiff, her stomach trembling with nervous dread. 'I said Charlie needs——'

'No, not that. What did you say about me not wanting *you*?' James asked her impatiently.

She shifted her glance from his face to the bed, then away from it to the window. Her heart was hammering frantically against her ribs, she felt sick, her palms sticky, her head muzzy. Now, with the adrenalin running out, she was afraid of the humiliation she was about to suffer.

'I said I know you don't want me in your life,' she told him huskily. Her throat felt sore and tight. She couldn't look at him, even though she was conscious of him moving towards her.

When James took hold of her she tensed immediately, her shocked eyes betraying her emotions.

'Just what in hell are you talking about?' he demanded grimly. 'You know damn well that's not true. You even said to me that you knew why I'd come back from Australia *and* what I wanted. What kind of game are you trying to play with me, Win? Do you realise just what you're doing to me, coming here, telling me that Charlie…my son needs me, wants me, making me feel like hell because I know I just don't have the control over my emotions that would allow me to stay and not…? And you…standing there so cool and controlled, when you know…'

She, cool and controlled? Win stared at him. Couldn't he feel the way she was trembling, couldn't he see…couldn't he—— ?'

'For God's sake, Win, don't you know what it does to me to know that I've barely got the self-control to stop myself from taking hold of you right here and now and making love to you until——' James took a deep breath. 'No wonder Charlie doesn't want me around. He knows exactly how I feel about you, and knows that no matter how much I love him—and I do—the way I feel about you means that given just even half the chance I'd be back in your life so fast…'

Win could barely take in what he was saying. Almost as though he was unable to help himself and didn't even realise what he was doing as he spoke, the fingers gripping her arms had started to caress her skin in a compulsively rhythmic sensuality that was already clouding her reason. She could feel the heat coming off his skin, her body absorbing its message of arousal, her senses urging her to move closer to him; to press herself against him and cling to him.

'I love you, Win,' she heard him saying thickly. 'Oh, God, how I love you.'

'But you can't. You left me...you...there was someone else...'

'No, never. Oh, Tara wanted me all right, but I never wanted her, not even for a second. My big mistake was letting her know it. Another was being stupid enough to get drunk and agreeing to let her take me home. I thought she meant home to you. It gave me one of the biggest shocks I've ever had in my life to wake up in her bed, in her flat...' He saw her face and grimaced. 'Nothing happened.'

'How do you know that? If you were drunk...'

'It's because I was so drunk that I know nothing *could* have happened,' he told her drily.

'But you let me divorce you! You never even tried...'

'Oh, Win.' His hands cupped her face, smoothing the soft skin, the expression on his face changing, his eyes darkening as he touched her mouth. 'If I kiss you now, I'm never going to be able to stop,' he told her huskily. 'I can't go on like this, not even for Charlie's sake. I...I love you too much. Don't you see? It's best for all of us if I go back. You already know what's all too likely to happen if I stay around. I have to go.'

'But... but I want you to stay,' Win told him.

They stared at one another. Win could feel the too rapid thud of her heart.

'For Charlie's sake,' James agreed bitterly.

She shook her head.

'No,' she told him huskily, 'for my own. I... I've never stopped loving you, James.'

'Never stopped?' He gave her a sardonic look. 'You never did love me, Win—how could you? You were only a child. God, will I ever be free of the guilt of loving you? I ruined your life,' he told her soberly. 'I loved you so much and so selfishly that I ignored everything everyone told me. That you were too young, too immature, that if I really loved you I'd stand back a little and give you some time to finish growing up—that I wouldn't use your sexual desire for me to bind you in a relationship which you weren't really ready for.'

Win stared at him.

'What are you saying? It wasn't like that. I *wanted* to marry you.'

'You wanted to have sex with me,' he told her brutally, then groaned when he saw her face. 'Win... Win, that's nothing to be ashamed of. If those brothers of yours hadn't been so damned protective you'd have learned long before you met me just how powerful the human sexual urge can be, but because of the way they'd guarded you, because of the way you'd been brought up, you could only accept your own sexuality and its needs by telling yourself that wanting me sexually must mean you loved me.

'*I* knew that, but I chose to ignore it. That was my fault...my guilt and not yours. I should have given you more time, been your lover before we were married; allowed you to discover your own sexuality and then to decide whether or not you wanted me emotionally, but I was so afraid of losing you that I didn't do that. I married you.'

'I *wanted* to marry you,' she protested.

'At first,' he agreed. 'But you soon changed your mind, didn't you? And then I had to go and make you pregnant. I've never forgiven myself for that.'

'*You've* never forgiven yourself!' Win exclaimed.

'You were a child—a child with a woman's body that was carrying the burden of my child.'

'I was *nineteen*,' she told him.

'I'm not talking about your age, Win. You were still very, very young. I hated myself for what I'd done to you, for my lack of care, for not making sure it couldn't happen, and yet at the same time... Oh, God, I wanted you so much—both of you.'

Win could hardly believe what she was hearing.

'But you hated my being pregnant. You could hardly bear to look at me. And in bed . . .'

'It wasn't *you* I hated,' James told her. 'It was me. I hated myself.'

'But you were so angry when Charlie was born. When he cried, when . . .'

'Not with you, Win, but again with myself, because he was a burden you shouldn't have had. Your family thought so as well, and I couldn't blame them. When you said you didn't love me any more and that you wanted a divorce, I knew they'd been right. I felt as though I'd cheated you of your youth, your freedom. I couldn't live with that knowledge any more, so I gave you your divorce, and I kept away from you and Charlie so that you could make a fresh life for yourselves, so that you could make your own choices. It was the hardest thing I've ever had to do, and it didn't get any better.

'"Mum and Dad sent me photographs, your own family wrote to me, and with each year that passed I missed you even more. Then when Charlie was six my parents sent me a letter he'd written to me—a Christmas card he'd made for me, and I couldn't . . . I had to get in touch with him, with you.'

Win swallowed. She remembered that Christmas. It had been just before James's parents had retired and moved away. Charlie had been asking her about James, and she had answered his questions as honestly as she could.

She remembered how she had cried when he'd shown her the card he had made at school for 'his daddy', and how relieved she had been when it disappeared.

'So know you know just why I can't stay. Not even for Charlie's sake. I'm simply incapable of staying and keeping out of your life. I was as jealous as hell over your hotel owner—far more jealous than poor Charlie could ever be. Somewhere deep inside me a part of me refuses to accept that you aren't mine.'

'That's funny,' Win told him softly, 'because a part of *me* feels exactly the same way.'

James looked at her for a long time, doubt, hesitation, and, most heart-shakingly of all, hope and love visible in his eyes.

Very slowly, her heart racing, Win raised herself up on her toes and placed her hands on either side of his face. She held him tenderly and then, much as though he were Charlie suffering the pain of some small physical wound, she stroked his skin and kissed him gently.

Only he wasn't Charlie, and suddenly kissing him gently wasn't what she wanted to do at all.

She was shaking as she opened her mouth over his and ran the tip of her tongue over his lips. She had never done this before, never taken the initiative, and for a moment she thought she had done the wrong thing and that she had simply imagined him saying he loved and wanted her.

But then she felt him tremble and his arms went round her, holding her as he kissed her, their bodies moving urgently together.

It was a long time before he stopped kissing her, and even then she kept her mouth close to his, teasing him with light biting caresses as he asked her, 'Charlie...where...?'

'Charlie's fine,' she told him firmly. 'He's spending the night with Heather.' She saw the look in his eyes and laughed, even while she could feel the colour running up under his skin. 'No,'she told him as she saw him glancing over her head at the bed, 'not here. Let's go home.'

Home, to make love in the same bed—the same room where they had first been lovers. The same bed where he had taken her the night Charlie had had his nightmare, the same bed where she had left him feeling as though her whole world had been shattered by the knowledge that she loved him.

They undressed one another slowly and lovingly, lingering over caresses that were familiar and unfamiliar, touching, tasting, letting their need build secure in the knowledge that they would find fulfilment in each other; that it wasn't just this night they would have together but all the nights and all the days for the rest of their lives.

They made love with passion and tears, with shared memories and loving laughter sharing their thoughts, their feelings, their needs, in a way that Win had never dreamed could be possible.

It was ten o'clock when James slowly and reluctantly released her.

'Would you like to go and get Charlie?' he asked her.

Win looked at him for a long time.

'Yes,' she admitted honestly. 'But we aren't going to. This night is ours, James,' she told him softly. 'Yours and mine, our bridge between our shared past and our future. Something to...'

'To sustain us for what lies ahead?' James suggested, kissing her. 'You know Charlie isn't going to be happy, don't you?'

'Not at first,' she agreed. 'But you are his father, James.'

'Yes, but you're his mother, and when you and I are remarried and he realises that I'm going to be here full time...'

Win's heart skipped a little over that 're-married'. Idiotic in this day and age to acknowledge how much that meant to her.

'But we will make it work?' she asked him, suddenly anxious, and a little insecure.

'Oh, yes,' he told her, 'we will make it work. Now come here and let me reassure myself that this isn't all some kind of dream. Mm...no, you *feel* real enough,' he told her as she complied, loving the warm glide of his hand against her skin, rubbing her face lovingly against his chest and then turning to kiss him, teasing him a little

with the delicate probe of her tongue as she slowly
circled the hard flat disc of his nipple, smiling as
she felt his sudden tension and knew that she was
arousing him.

'You know what's going to happen if you don't
stop that, don't you?' he warned, groaning the
words against her ear so that their reverberation
made her shiver a little.

'No,' she lied, trailing soft kisses up towards
his throat, tantalised by the pulse she could see
throbbing beneath his skin. 'Show me.'

Win needed her memories of that night to draw
on and sustain her many times over the following
months.

Charlie did not react well when she told him
that she and James were to remarry, and there
were many, many times when she feared that
James might change his mind, marvelling at his
patience with Charlie. A patience she suspected
that, had their positions been reversed, she could
never have shown.

And then, just two weeks before they were due
to be married, Charlie ran away from home.

It was James who found him trying to hitch a
ride on the approach to the motorway; James
who brought him back; James who talked to him
and James who comforted him when he broke
down in tears, bewildered by his own emotions
and fears.

That was the only time Win felt even tempted to call the wedding off, and not for Charlie's sake but for James's, but James counselled her to be patient just a little while longer and to give Charlie time to overcome his own inner battle with himself.

'He loves us both,' he told Win. 'But he's always had you to himself, and part of him still doesn't want to share you with anyone else.'

'But to try to blackmail me into giving you up by running away like that...'

'The male sex is like that,' James told her drily. 'Especially when motivated by jealousy.'

It was a quiet wedding, all of them subdued, with no honeymoon afterwards. Later James planned to take them all away for a family holiday, but right now he was busy with the new business.

Charlie was slowly distancing himself from Win, and while part of her was glad, another part of her felt unbearable guilt for having driven him away.

He was maturing so quickly, growing taller, his voice starting to break. He was not a child any longer at all, but she worried secretly about how her remarriage to James would affect his life, and how his attitude to James would affect their marriage.

Outwardly now he seemed to accept James, but inwardly...

And, as if that weren't enough, Win was feeling increasingly unwell, losing weight, feeling sick and dizzy, and feeling so tired that everything, even making love, somehow seemed to require a tremendous effort.

She told Heather.

'You're not pregnant, are you?' Heather asked her thoughtfully.

Pregnant? For some reason that possibility had never even occurred to her. How could *she*, the mother of an almost fourteen-year-old son, be pregnant?

Very easily, it seemed, and for the second time in her life she found herself dreading having to announce her condition. Not to James—instinctively she knew with what love and delight James would welcome her news.

But Charlie... How on earth was Charlie going to react?

She had to tell him, of course, and before it became obvious to others that she was pregnant. The last thing she wanted was for him to learn about it second hand.

'Right, Zoe, it's bedtime for you.'

Win hid a small grin at the look of awe on the face of the girl, watching as Charlie swept his two-year-old sister up off the floor, handling her with the kind of expertise that only came from long practice.

'I'll do that, Charlie,' she told him, starting to stand up, but Charlie shook his head.

'No, Mum, you stay where you are. Dad will never forgive me if you go into labour early this time as well. After all, he nearly missed out on Zoe's birth.'

Win sank back into her chair. In truth she *was* feeling rather tired—Zoe was a very exuberant two-year-old, rather advanced beyond her age, and right now, towards the end of her third pregnancy, Win was beginning to feel quite worn out.

Three years ago, if anyone had suggested to her that she might one day witness the present scene, she would never have believed it, which only went to show how much things could change.

All through her pregnancy with Zoe, Charlie had been difficult and withdrawn, and she had sympathised with him, knowing how hard it was for him, but then she had gone into labour a couple of weeks early, and Zoe had been so impatient to arrive that Win had had to rely on Charlie to summon the ambulance and to take charge.

He had gone with her right into the delivery-room, no one realising in the mild panic of her unexpected arrival that he was actually there, and then, once they had realised, a junior nurse had been dispatched to take him to the waiting-room.

He hadn't wanted to go, and, even in the travail of giving birth to Zoe, Win had seen the panic and fear in his eyes. She had wanted to call out to the nurse to let him stay, but Zoe was growing very impatient and, when she'd next had time to concentrate on anything but helping her daughter into the world, miraculously James had arrived and was holding her hand. What she *hadn't* realised until she heard him saying calmly, 'You come and stand here, Charlie, and hold your mum's hand,' was that Charlie was actually still in the room. Over his head her eyes had met James's and read the message in them.

'Yes, Charlie, hold my hand.'

She had smiled at them both while the midwife tut-tutted a little, but it had been a relatively easy birth, and Charlie was clinging so tightly to her hand that Win suspected it would have taken surgery to break his grip of her.

It was James who handed Zoe to Charlie, saying softly to her,

'You're very lucky, young lady—you know that, don't you? Without Charlie here...'

Charlie wasn't listening. He was staring in fascination at her, measuring the smallness of her hand against his own.

Zoe was the star of Charlie's year's parenting skills class at school that summer, and Charlie had quickly become an expert on how babies were to be brought up. A little to Win's own chagrin, it wasn't *her* at whom Zoe smiled first, but Charlie.

It was also that summer that Charlie had told
her he had been afraid she might die while she
was having Zoe and that he might lose her. Win's
heart ached as she held him.

'It's very rare for anything like that to happen
these days, Charlie,' she told him gently.

'Oh, yeah, I know that now. I mean, I was
there, wasn't I, when she was born——'

Win opened her mouth to tell him that Zoe's
had been a particularly easy and speedy birth,
then closed it again.

'Yes, you were there,' she agreed softly.

'And now we're a real family,' Charlie added.

A real family. Tears stung her eyes, but she
suppressed them.

After this new baby there were definitely not
going to be any more, she and James had decided. This one would be a companion for Zoe
and, they hoped, would ensure that she did not
grow up to be too spoiled and indulged. Not by
James and herself; she had learned her lesson
with Charlie.

No, it was Charlie who was in danger of
spoiling Zoe. Already she could wind him around
her little finger. A little bit of healthy sibling
rivalry would do her the world of good, Win decided as she heard her daughter call out imper-
iously, 'Charlie, Charlie! Read me! Read me!'

His poor girlfriend didn't stand a chance, Win
decided as she got up after all and went upstairs,

to tell her daughter that Charlie had more important things to do than read bedtime stories to her.

'No, not you,' Zoe told her firmly. 'Want Charlie.'

'Charlie has homework to do,' Win told her comfortably, ignoring her wail of protest, chuckling a little to herself.

'What's amusing you?' James asked her, coming into Zoe's bedroom behind her.

'Nothing really. I was just reflecting how much easier it is second time around.'

'Easy? I wouldn't say that,' James murmured, wrapping his arms around her and kissing the nape of her neck.

'Not this. Us,' Win told him lovingly, turning round to return his kiss. 'I meant children...Zoe. I meant... Mm...'

She stopped speaking as James continued to kiss her. After all, she could explain to him what she had meant later. Much later, she decided as she switched out Zoe's light and gently opened the bedroom door.

HARLEQUIN®

PRESENTS
RELUCTANT BRIDEGROOMS

Two beautiful brides, two unforgettable romances...
two men running for their lives....

My Lady Love, by Paula Marshall, introduces
Charles, Viscount Halstead, who lost his memory
and found himself employed as a stableboy by the
untouchable Nell Tallboys, Countess Malplaquet.
But Nell didn't consider Charles untouchable—
not at all!

Darling Amazon, by Sylvia Andrew, is the story of
a spurious engagement between Julia Marchant
and Hugo, marquess of Rostherne—an engagement
that gets out of hand and just may lead Hugo to
the altar after all!

Enjoy two madcap Regency weddings this May,
wherever Harlequin books are sold.

REG5

HARLEQUIN PRESENTS®

We're not keeping it to ourselves!
Secrets...
**The exciting collection of intriguing, sensual stories
from Harlequin Presents**

Everyone Has Something To Hide

Trail of Love by Amanda Browning

Harlequin Presents #1742

Kay Napier was a happy, intelligent young woman who had
been brought up in a loving home. Then lightning struck.
The first bolt came in the disturbingly attractive shape of
Ben Radford. The second was a challenge to her very identity.
It was unsettling to discover that she wasn't who she thought
she was. But nothing as unnerving as finding that Ben wanted
her body, but not her love. And to prove that, Ben intended to
marry someone else....

Available in May wherever Harlequin books are sold.

An affair...with her own husband? Laura and Dirk had
been separated but, all of a sudden, he was back in her
life and pursuing her. Laura couldn't forget that she had
been unable to conceive Dirk's child, which meant there
could be no long-term future for them—so why was she
still tempted to accept his simply *outrageous* proposal!

Nell was wary of men, until she met Ben Rigby and
found herself longing for something more. But she was
afraid. Her child—her lost child, whom she'd never had
the chance to see—shared the same birthday as Ben's
adopted son...was Fate being cruel or kind?

Harlequin Presents Plus—where
women's dreams come true!

Coming next month:

An Outrageous Proposal by Miranda Lee
Harlequin Presents Plus #1737

and

Shadow Play by Sally Wentworth
Harlequin Presents Plus #1738

Harlequin Presents Plus
The best has just gotten better!

Available in May wherever Harlequin books are sold.